MW01230863

# MOON OF THE WITCH

### BLACK BAYOU WITCH TALES BOOK 3

### LORI BEASLEY BRADLEY

# ACKNOWLEDGMENTS

I would like to thank my fabulous critique group, The Central Phoenix Writers' Workshop, for their excellent guidance and understanding.

Thanks also to HobNobs Coffee Shop, where we meet every Wednesday night. The food and atmosphere are great, and the people are lovely.

I would also like to say thank you to my dear friend Adam Sterling for keeping my nose to the grindstone and pointing out my bird tracks. I hope I've swept them all up.

My sister, Jodi Nelson, deserves plenty of thanks for pushing me toward a paranormal romance. It was out of my comfort zone, but she said I could do it. I hope you like it, Sis. If we are not open to trying new things, we never grow.

I also must thank all of you who buy my work. I write because I love telling you all a story. Thank you for allowing me to do that.

This is a work of fiction, and any errors in details fall squarely upon me.

Dalton La Pierre sat with every nerve ending in his body shooting off storm warnings. He nervously stared across the table from his date, Althea Rubidoux. Watching her face intently for that first spark of anger in her enchanting dark eyes, Dalton wondered how he would break up with her without dodging dishes and flatware. How should he begin this conversation? You're lovely, Althea, but you're an absolute bitch? No, that probably wouldn't be the way to go if he wanted to keep his eyes.

Althea Rubidoux was physically beautiful beyond belief. Dalton had been surprised eight months earlier when the honey-skinned mulatto woman accepted his first invitation to dinner. Now he sat at another dinner with her, wondering how to cut her loose. It just went to prove true what his grandpa used to say: Be careful what you wish for, boy because you might just get it.

Dalton drove a tow truck and parted out old cars for a living. Why would the most beautiful woman in St. Elizabeth, Louisiana, go out with a simple grease-monkey when she could go into New Orleans and have her choice of more substantial men?

But Althea had accepted his invitation to dinner at Le Petit Paris Café in St. Elizabeth, where they'd both grown up and attended school. Dalton knew the tall beauty on sight, but he'd never thought he'd stood a chance with her back in high school against all the rich townies and jocks. Ten years since high school and the owner of his own wrecker and parts business, Dalton thought he might give it a try with the leggy woman.

He'd caught a call one afternoon for a motorist in distress on the highway outside town and found that motorist to be Althea Rubidoux. It looked to Dalton as though a water hose on her expensive Mercedes had blown, and Althea stood, leaning upon the front fender of the steaming automobile. She wore a clingy black jumpsuit and strappy open-toed heels. Althea was the picture of desirability with her exposed cleavage and tawny skin accentuated by the sexy plunging neckline of the clingy garment. Her wavy black hair hung loose to her waist, and her pouty red lips shone in the waning sunlight over the Black Bayou.

Dalton's penis had sprung to life at just the thought of her, but seeing her standing there dressed up like a supermodel getting ready to hit the runway had been more than he could bear. Dalton smiled and adjusted his jeans in an attempt to mask his throbbing erection.

"Hey there, Althea," Dalton had greeted her, removing his grease-stained ball cap to run his hand through his sandy-blonde curls. "The Benz take a shit on ya?"

"Seems so," Althea said flatly, but moved in a manner that exposed her ample breasts provocatively in Dalton's direction.

"Well, get in and pop the hood for me so I can see what's goin' on under there."

"Sure thing," Althea said, flashing bright, white even teeth. She turned and swayed her shapely behind as she walked gracefully back to open the door of the car and drop unceremoniously into the deep bucket seat.

Dalton heard the hood release as he pulled on leather work-gloves in order to lift it. Steam billowed into his face as he did so.

He could tell at first glance that Althea's fancy foreign car had lost a water hose. Dalton couldn't tell whether or not the hose was completely missing or only disconnected without digging a little deeper, but it would be an easy fix even if the hose proved to be gone. He carried several on his truck, as well as the necessary clamps. Dalton rooted around a little and found the water hose unclamped and hanging at one end, draining the water from Althea's automobile.

"I got ya covered," Dalton yelled from under the hood as he clamped the hose back into place. "It's just a loose hose. As soon as I get this clamp tightened back up, I'll refill her with water," he yelled but gave a start when he looked up to see Althea bending over the car and staring into the steamy engine compartment as Dalton worked. "You see, just a hose. No biggy."

Althea leaned over the car to give Dalton a clear view of her plump breasts, and her nipples erect beneath the flimsy black fabric. "You're good with your hands," she said, flashing the smile again. "You like what you see—Dalton, isn't it? Dalton La Pierre?"

Dalton tried to concentrate on the job at hand. "Yes ... I mean, yes, it's Dalton. We were in school together. You were in my Junior English Lit class with old lady Hillshire."

"Yes, of course, of course. I liked the old bird," Althea said, fluttering her thick black lashes at him as he sweated over the hot engine.

"She was alright, I suppose," Dalton said, "but she made us write too many essays about stuff like *The Old Man and the Sea* and *Moby Dick*. I think the old gal had a thing about the ocean or something."

"I always liked the way she engaged us with stories about the authors' personal lives, like their sexual orientations and stuff like that." Althea leaned in a little farther, exposing more of her beautiful breast.

"Yeah," Dalton agreed, trying to ignore the sweaty throbbing between his thighs. "She did make it interesting, and none of that crap ever showed up on the tests, either." Althea agreed and laughed with him.

They stood talking that way for over an hour, about classes and classmates. Then Dalton got enough nerve up to make his move. "Would you like to go to dinner tomorrow night?" He blurted out the question. "We could go to Le Petit Paris for steaks or someplace else if you want."

"Le Petit Paris would be wonderful. I love their gumbo." She dug into her black leather clutch and pulled out a glossy business card. "Here's my card with my address here in town and my number. Shall we say seven, then?"

"Sure," Dalton mumbled, taking the card, and shoving it into the breast pocket of his sweaty, grease-stained t-shirt. "I'll see you at seven."

Althea grabbed his hand. Dalton thought his heart would stop in that instant. "Wait a minute. What do I owe you for the service call?"

"Nothing," he said, waving her off. "It was just a silly hose. I only had to replace the clamp and refill her with water. No charge for that." For anyone else, it would have been a thirty-five dollar charge, but not for Althea Rubidoux with those amazing breasts.

After that first dinner, Dalton and Althea had dated regularly for over eight months. Their lovemaking had been beyond anything Dalton could have imagined, but something about Althea, her family, and her close friends rubbed Dalton the wrong way.

Most of them lived out in remote areas of the Black Bayou and were secretive about their goings-on. Dalton had gone to dinner at Althea's parents' place once, and, was surprised to find that the only way to their home was by boat. Her family lived in a creepy compound on an island in the middle of the Black Bayou.

Dalton remembered his grandpa telling him and his sister

that the island was haunted, and to never to go out there. He had no idea that people actually lived out on the rocky mound in the center of all that mist. When Dalton had asked about Althea's family ancestry and how long they had been in the bayou, her father acted evasive and her mother sat nervously in silence.

Althea later told him the family had been on the island since around the time the first Acadians had settled the region, in the early Eighteenth Century. The secrecy still irked Dalton, and it was one of the reasons he now planned to end things with the beautiful woman sitting across the table from him. He didn't like secrets or spooky haunted islands in the middle of Black Bayou.

Dalton thought the island bread more bitches than anything else and that's what his grandpa should have warned him about rather than ghosts and other scary shit. Staring at the woman across the table from him now, Dalton couldn't think of anything scarier than Althea Rubidoux at her bitchiest.

"What's going on tonight, Dalton, honey?" Althea took his hands and smiled sweetly with her full lips and deep-set, dark eyes shining. "Is this a special occasion I don't know about?" He watched her thick dark lashes flutter in anticipation of his answer.

Sensing he may find himself in trouble, Dalton broke free of Althea's grasp and shrugged. "Nothing special," he said too quickly. "I just thought we should talk." He hesitated, nervously glancing around the busy café. "And I thought this would be a good place to do it."

Althea's eyes narrowed. Dalton sensed trouble coming. "Are *you* dumping *me*, Dalton La Pierre?" Althea asked hotly. Dalton thanked his stars that she said it quietly and not in her regular loud screech.

Althea's fiery temper had proven to be a problem with Dalton. While he enjoyed their sexual relationship immensely, he couldn't tolerate her rants at the tiniest presumed infraction on his part. He'd pulled her, screaming and fighting, from many an establishment in St. Elizabeth.

Her senseless rants in public places embarrassed him, while Althea didn't seem to be embarrassed at all. That irked Dalton. His mother had taught him to be respectful of others in public, and he didn't like being made a spectacle of.

"Althea, we haven't really been seeing eye-to-eye for a while now." A waiter brought them wine and poured the sweet red liquid into large glasses on delicate stems. "I think we should take a little break for a while, and let things settle down. Maybe we should see other people?" He picked up his wine glass and gulped some of it down.

"See other people?" She narrowed her eyes again, and Dalton recognized the storm about to hit as the tone of her voice raised an octave. "Have you been steppin' out on *me*, you ridiculous, greasy wrench-jockey? Just who in hell do you think *you* are to do that to *me*?" Wine soon ran down Dalton's face as he watched Althea's backside pass through the door onto the patio, and he cringed as he heard her kicking around the metal patio furniture.

A waiter handed him a towel with an amused grin. "I don't suppose you'll be ordering dinner then?"

"No, I don't suppose so," Dalton replied with a sheepish grin. He finished wiping wine from his hazel eyes and dropped the wine-stained towel onto the table. "Sorry for the mess and the disruption." Dalton handed the waiter his credit card to pay for the wine.

"No worries," the young man said with a smile. "Men have brought Miss Althea here to break up before. It always turns out pretty much the same way." He took Dalton's card, ran it, and brought back the receipt to be signed. Dalton added a five-dollar tip and left the little Café, stepping out into the warm, damp air that smelled of the swamp.

Another reason Dalton had decided to make a break with Althea had been his new relationship with Julia DuBois, a perky little redhead who worked as a drive-thru teller at his bank. They'd struck up a conversation one afternoon while she worked on one of the transfer units, trying to dislodge a carrier stuck in the vacuum tube.

After dealing with Althea and her cartwheeling moods, Julia soothed him like a fresh, cool breeze off the bayou in summer. She struck Dalton as sweet and easy-going. Their first date had been burgers and onion rings in his pick-up at the Sonic on the edge of town. Sonic burgers in Dalton's messy truck would never have been a dinner date he'd have considered broaching with Althea.

Dalton parked his truck in front of Julia's white clapboard cottage and got out. The heady scents of jasmine and honey-suckle met his nose upon leaving his vehicle, carrying bags of pulled pork with slaw and fries. He knew Julia would have Bud Longnecks in her fridge. Dalton knocked on the door and smiled when the bubbly redhead answered, wearing denim shorts and a tight-fitting tank top without a bra.

"Hey Jules," he lifted the greasy brown paper bags. "I brought supper."

"I thought you were going to be otherwise engaged tonight." Julia rolled her big green eyes as she pushed the screened door open. "Get on in here with that bag. I'm famished and it smells delicious."

"You just happened to know I'd be showin' up with food in hand?" He asked playfully as he stepped over her threshold. The door slapped his firm behind on the way in as it closed.

Julia took the bags. "Miss Althea Rubidoux does not take rejection well. Everybody in town knows that, Dalton." Julia laughed, then disappeared into the kitchen with the food. "Are you telling me that you didn't?" She called to him with a bubbly giggle.

He sighed and rolled his hazel eyes. "I suppose I should have, huh?"

---

## 2

"Jules, you're such an amazin' woman." Dalton bent and kissed her soft, warm lips. "You're just so comfortable to be with." He ran his hand through her bright red curls as he pulled her head into the curve of his big body, made muscular by years of physical labor.

"Dalton La Pierre, are you comparing me to an old pair of shoes?" Julia asked with mock sarcasm and popped the last fry into her mouth.

"That's exactly how I feel about you, Jules," Dalton said with a wide grin on his square-jawed face. "It's the same way I feel about my old Red Wings." He playfully ruffled her curls with his big hand. "I actually like to think of you as fitting like a pair of my comfortable old jeans, though. That's the part of you I love wrapped around me the most." He unbuttoned his cotton shirt and shrugged it off his shoulders.

"Oh, yeah?" she swatted at his broad, bare chest. "I just bet it is." Julia smiled up at him warmly. "I kind of like being down there, myself." She stretched up a small, freckled hand to caress his smooth cheek and caught the briefest scent of his spicy after-shave. "You do realize that you just used the 'L' word, don't you?"

"Babe, I love that part of all women, not just you." Dalton tipped up his Bud and swallowed down a quarter of the bottle. He shut his eyes tight, wondering how he'd gotten himself in trouble with yet another woman so quickly. His grandpa would have boxed his ear for being such a fool. "I love other parts of you too, Jules. You have really great tits, your green eyes are really, really pretty, and your curly mop of hair is real pretty, too." He tapped the tip of her freckled snub nose with his index finger in jest.

"Well, at least you're honest." Julia pulled his head down to hers, and their lips met in a passionate kiss. She wrapped her hands around his neck, pulling him gently into her face. She tasted his sweet, salty mouth with the hint of brewer's yeast and smoky bar-b-que sauce on his probing tongue as it twined around hers.

His rough hand found her breasts under the tank top she wore and rolled her nipples into erect mounds of flesh between his thumb and forefinger. "Like I said before, nice tits, firm and very responsive." He pulled the cotton top up and over Julia's head and brought his mouth down to suck a nipple between his teeth. He bit lightly, teasing.

"Oh, Dalton, honey," Julia gasped with each nibble, "don't stop, babe. That feels so good." He sucked harder and slid his right hand down over her flat belly to fumble with the snap and zipper on her shorts. Once open, Dalton slipped his hand in to find her wet crevasse.

"Oh, yeah. Finger me good. Massage my clit. It's throbbing like crazy." She gasped. "It wants you." He slid a second finger inside Julia's vagina. He grasped her pulsing clit between them, slowly working the fingers back and forth over her throbbing, engorged bundle of nerves until she moaned and thrust her hips up to meet his probing fingers. Julia reached for his snap and zipper but found them already open. She gently reached in and released his throbbing erection. Her petit hand encircled the pulsing organ and squeezed.

"That feels so good, Jules. Jack me with that soft hand," he moaned out, pulling her over to lie on her back upon the throw rug in front of her couch. "I'm gonna take your shorts down now." Dalton yanked the petite woman's shorts down over her backside and past her thighs. When they got to her knees, Julia kicked the denim shorts free. She spread her legs, and Dalton rolled his long, lean body atop hers. He bent his head and kissed her mouth again. Dalton's muscles rippled across his upper arms and shoulders as he held the weight of his upper body with them.

His erection pushed toward Julia's wet, throbbing center. "Fuck me, honey," she begged and pulled his face into hers again. "Fuck me good." He shoved his meaty cock into her. "Oh, yeah. Give me all of it." Julia shivered as his erection slid in and out of her, rubbing up against her clit. She arched up into his thrusts and used the muscles in her vaginal walls to clinch and release him.

"Keep that up, Jules," he panted. "Don't stop. Ahhh," Dalton moaned. "It feels so damned good when you do that."

Julia brought her arms down to caress his heaving ass as he thrust into her. She used Dalton's weight to leverage her body and push into him as he shoved into her repeatedly. Soon they both exploded with exhausting orgasms.

"Oh my god, Dalton," Julia gasped and dug her nails into his muscular shoulders, "I'm cumming so good, babe."

"Me too, Jules." He gave one last hard shove with his release. His big body collapsed atop hers. Sweat ran from his forehead, and his damp hair turned into a mass of sandy-blonde ringlets. "Jesus, Jules. I swear it's better every time we fuck. I've never experienced this with any woman before," he whispered into Julia's ear. "A cum was just a cum, but this is amazing. I can't get enough of you." Dalton rolled off onto the floor beside her, panting.

Julia reached for her discarded top and shoved it between her legs to catch his fluid dripping from her vagina before it could mess the antique rug. She swatted Dalton's bare ass. "I sorta like it too. I couldn't have asked for a better dessert." She giggled with delight. Something caught Julia's eye, and she went silent as she peered intently at the window, looking out onto her front porch. She caught the fleeting reflection of eyes staring in at them. Startled, Julia wrapped her arms to cover her naked breasts and whispered, "Dalton, I think someone's watching us."

Dalton scrambled up onto the couch, grabbing his jeans. "What?" he asked in a hoarse whisper. "Where?" He began shoving his legs into his jeans as his eyes darted frantically between the two living room windows and the window in the front door.

"I saw eyes at the window," Julia told him, nodding slightly toward the front window.

Dalton strode to the window, parting the lace drapes. " Fucking Christ," he groaned out. Then he went to the front door and twisted the antique knob.

"What?" Julia exclaimed as she pulled on her shorts and wrapped herself in a throw from the couch. "Who is it?" she asked.

Dalton pulled open the door to reveal Althea Rubidoux standing outside in the glow of the porch light. "What the fuck, Althea?"

Althea pushed past Dalton, her dark eyes bright with tears of hurt and rage. "So this is the little bitch you've been fucking behind my back?" She stormed up to Julia and drew her arm back to strike the much shorter redhead. Dalton grabbed Althea's arm before she could deliver the blow. "That's enough, Althea." He turned the raging woman toward the opened door. "You need to go. You and I are over. I've had enough of your insane temper tantrums to last me a lifetime."

Althea shrugged off his hands, "*We* are far from *over*, Dalton. When *I'm* done with you, you'll know it beyond a doubt." She turned to Julia and pointed a tawny finger. "As for you, Sister, I'll have my satisfaction later. Upon the next moon, I'll have my satisfaction. So mote it be!" Althea turned and marched from the room, leaving Dalton and Julia standing together open-mouthed.

"What the hell was that all about?" Dalton asked with his brow furrowed in confusion. "What was she babbling about, getting satisfaction and calling you her sister? You aren't sisters, are you?"

"Not by blood," Julia sighed out. "We're Sisters of the Moon."

"What?" Dalton raised a thick blonde eyebrow. "What in hell's name are you talkin' about, Jules?"

Julia took a deep breath and sat down on the couch. "It's a long story." Julia patted the cushion beside her. "Come, sit down, and I'll try to explain."

Dalton stood staring down at Julia, running a hand through his sweat-damp curls. "I will, but I need another beer." He began to walk toward the kitchen. "How about you?"

"Sure, I'll have another." Julia stood up and let the velour throw fall from her shoulders onto the couch. "I'm gonna put on a robe." She bent and picked up her messed tank top to throw into the hamper and walked to her bedroom. There, she pitched the soiled top to join her other dirty clothes and grabbed a robe from the hook on the bedroom door. She slowly walked back into the living room, pulling the tie to her silky robe tight at her waist.

Dalton sat on the couch with a beer bottle in his hand. Julia joined him, taking his hand into hers. "This is all going to sound pretty weird to you, and you're probably going to think I'm out of my ever-lovin' mind."

"What?" Dalton asked with his face screwed up in confusion. His long lashes fluttered over his confused eyes.

Julia took a pull on her beer then plunged ahead. "All right, here goes," she said, and exhaled a deep breath. "Althea and I are both Sisters of the Moon. We're what you'd call witches." Julia watched his face for a reaction.

"What do you mean by witches? Pointy hats and flying on

broomsticks?" He stared at Julia with a creased forehead. "That's nonsense. What are you talkin' about?"

"It's not nonsense, Dalton." Julia took another sip from her amber glass bottle. "Althea and I both practice witchcraft. Our *families* practice witchcraft and have been members of covens here in the bayou for centuries now. The Rubidoux Coven lives out on that island in the Black Bayou, and the DuBois Coven all live in and around town here. It's been that way since the families migrated down here from Canada in 1712. They were running from religious persecution. They tortured, hung, and burned witches back then, you know. Remember what they did in Salem."

"But that was just a bunch of crazy teenage girls, crying witch to get attention. None of those women were really witches." He looked into Julia's eyes intently. "Were they?"

"I can't say for certain, but probably not. Most of the practicing families had fled to Canada long before that."

"You're really serious, aren't you? You actually think you're a witch, don't you?" Dalton smiled and touched a finger to the end of Julia's nose. "Do you wiggle your cute little nose and make things appear and disappear like that old show on TV?"

"No," Julia said and smiled. "We don't do that, but we do cast spells. It's more like a religion than anything else. Some people go to church, say prayers, and sing hymns to their God. We go out into the forest to our alters, cast spells, and chant to our Goddess."

"What do you mean by 'we'? How many people around here think they're witches?"

"There are almost thirty in my coven. It's mainly close and extended family." Julia's face darkened. "Althea's coven is a little bigger, and they're a little different from us."

"You mean, like how Baptists are different from Catholics?" Dalton asked, scratching his head.

"Something like that. The DuBois Coven has always practiced white magic. We do healing spells and that sort of thing.

13

The Rubidoux Coven, on the other hand, has mainly practiced dark magic. They make and sell curses."

"You mean like voodoo dolls and love potions?" He laughed.

"Don't laugh," Julia snapped. "It's not a laughing matter. Our coven's healing magic cured Mary Taylor of her cancer when the doctors had given up, and I'm fairly certain Althea's Coven caused Marc Thibodeaux's car accident last year. He pissed off Althea's dad over some business deal." Julia took a deep breath. "There's a good reason why nobody dares to cross the Rubidoux family in St. Elizabeth. They killed six people in that accident. It wiped out the entire family, and nobody's seen Marc's cousin since after the funerals. Nobody knows what happened to him."

"How could they cause an accident? Did they shoot out that tire and put the tree in the way for the car to hit?" Dalton took Julia's hand. "Jules, it was just an accident, or maybe the cousin did something to their car and ran away afterward. People can't make accidents happen. They're acts of God."

"Exactly, but you have your God, and we have ours. My coven and I chant to Artemis and Demeter. I think Althea and her coven chant directly to Hades. They incant only to the darkest gods."

Dalton shook his head. "I'm not going to pretend to understand any of this, but if it's what you believe, I'm not going to condemn it. This is America, and you can worship any way or any god you like."

Julia threw her arms around his neck and kissed his firm lips. "Thanks for understanding, babe, and not calling me a total nutcase." Julia loosened the tie on her robe, exposing her shapely white breasts. "Shall we retire to my room?"

Dalton smiled. "You'd better believe it, Witchypoo," he said as he took her hand and let Julia lead him down the hall to her bedroom.

---

## 3

D alton tossed and turned. Unbelievable pain wracked his body, and he burned with a raging fever. At times he lay on the cool, muddy bank of the Vermillion River feeding the bayou, and then he'd smell something warm and savory like the juices from a rare steak on his tougue. The scent would make his mouth water, and he'd begin running. He couldn't understand why he ran or why he chased the scent, but the compulsion spurred him on.

He had to have what he chased. A furious rage consumed him. When he possessed his quarry, he'd tear it apart, ripping it limb from limb until it stopped moving. Dalton could only see red. He wanted to taste blood. He wanted to have that hot wet fluid. He wanted to smell it, taste it, and roll in it.

He thrashed and rolled. Sweat poured into his eyes. He wiped at them, but he couldn't get out the salty sweat. It stung, and it burned. The pain returned. He howled. and shook. Something crushed him and pulled him. His body was being turned inside out. It felt as though his internal organs were being stretched, then compressed and stretched again.

Then it all stopped. The mind-numbing pain ended. The

fever cooled, and his body now shivered with a chill. His eyes continued to sting, and Dalton opened them, expecting to see in the bedroom, darkened by the blackout drapes at his windows. He expected to be waking in his bed after experiencing a horrific nightmare, but he blinked bright sunlight from his eyes and raised his hand up to shield them.

Dalton was struck with horror when he saw his hands. Crusting red blood coated his fingers and his palms. He held them before his face and turned them slowly to inspect the caked blood. The coppery tang filled his nostrils and coated his tongue. Noting stiffness on his cheeks, Dalton used a bloody hand to wipe away drying blood from his face. What the hell had happened to him?

Someone laughed insanely nearby. He wiped his eyes and studied his surroundings. When he sat up he realized that he was in a grassy field lined with tall oaks and sweet gums. On the stump of an old cypress sat Althea Rubidoux wrapped in black velvet. She turned her head toward Dalton and began to laugh again. Standing, she then walked to where Dalton sat naked and shivering.

"Well, it's about time," she sneered. "I thought for a while there that you were going to sleep 'til noon."

"Where am I, and what am I doing here covered in blood, Althea?" Dalton scratched at the drying blood caking his arm. "What did you do to me?"

"It wasn't just me, you stupid man," Althea hissed. Her black hair drifted about her shoulders in the soft morning breeze. "My coven helped. It's a complicated ritual and takes more than one witch to accomplish it."

"What in hell's name are you talking about?" Dalton demanded. "Don't tell me you're actually into that witch bull-shit, too." Dalton attempted to stand, but his arms and legs hurt like hell. They felt weak and wouldn't carry his body. He fell back to the ground.

"It will take a while to get your bearings after your first change."

"Change? What the hell, Althea. What did you and your bunch of black magic witches do to me?"

"So, your bitch has been running her mouth about secret things, I see. She'll pay for that, too."

"For Christ's sake, tell me what you drugged me with and help me up." Dalton reached a bloody limb out to the laughing woman in black.

Althea slapped his hand away. "Get yourself to your feet, Dalton. Now I'm done with you and you can figure it out on your own from here on out."

"Just tell me what you drugged me with, bitch and how long it'll take to clear my system," Dalton growled.

"I didn't drug you, sugar. I put a curse on you. You are now *loup-garou*, Dalton," Althea laughed as she saw the horror dawn on his face. "Yes, my lover, you will change into a wolf creature with every full moon to hunt and kill. The *loup-garou* is driven to kill by his insatiable desire for blood. You will wake like this, naked and bloody after each full moon. Your body will ache from the change, and your heart will ache from the horror of the murders you commit during the night." She smiled a hideous smile. "The *loup-garou* craves human blood above all else," she said, and turned away from him.

Dalton sat cross-legged in the grass with his head in his hands. He remained that way until cold water dumped over his head shocked him from a half-daze. "What the hell," he shouted, sputtering and wiping bloody water from his eyes.

"Let's get with it, La Pierre," a man's voice from behind ordered. "I've got to get you back to town before it's time to leave for work." Another bucket of water drenched him. A dry towel landed on his head, and someone dropped a pile of clothes beside him. "Wipe off and get dressed." Dalton looked up to see Jerry LaMonte, a checker at the local Wal-Mart, and an acquaintance from his gym class in high school.

"What the hell, Jerry?" Dalton snarled. "You part of this witch bullshit too?"

"It's not bullshit, man," the skinny man, wearing thick horn-rimmed glasses and a blue Wal-Mart vest sneered, "and you sure as hell shouldn't have pissed off Althea like you did. It looks like you're not the hotshot you were in gym class anymore." Jerry snickered. "You're gonna have to disappear into the bayou like all the others who've pissed her off." He rolled his eyes, made to look larger by the thick lenses of his glasses. "Maybe you can be the top-dog of the pack out there," he said with a grin on his pock-marked face. Dalton remembered Jerry catching a lot of hell in high school because of his terrible acne.

"If it's not a bunch of bullshit, why didn't you get your magical buddies to fix your eyes and clean up your pimples?"

"Shut-up, La Pierre," Jerry said, kicking the pile of clothes, "and put on the sweats so I can get my ass to work on time."

Dalton wanted to come back with something hurtful, but he couldn't think of anything. His grandpa had taught him better than that. He pulled on the gray sweats and stood on unsteady legs.

"I've heard the change hurts like hell and that you're sore for days afterward," Jerry said almost sympathetically, and offered Dalton his arm for support. "My truck is over here. It's not far."

Dalton took the offered arm and used it as they walked to Jerry's pickup, parked behind a stand of sweet gums hung with sphagnum moss. The stringy moss looked like the tangled strands of an old woman's hair as it danced in the light breeze.

"Thanks," Dalton said as he slid carefully into the passenger side of the old truck. The old Ford smelled of stale beer from the discarded beer bottles on the floorboard Dalton had to kick out of his way and cigarette butts in the overfull ashtray made him gag. "What's up with all of this?" Dalton asked when Jerry got in behind the wheel.

"Well, you ended up on the wrong end of an evil curse." Jerry started the truck and shifted it into gear.

"Is there anything to be done about it?" Dalton shifted his weight, trying to find a comfortable position on the hard bench seat. "I mean, like, an antidote or something."

"I think there is," Jerry said and shifted into a higher gear as they traveled down a gravel road toward town, "but I'm pretty sure it's complicated, and you'd need another strong witch and a coven to perform the ritual to reverse what we did. Althea said you're fucking one of the DuBois women. You should get one of them. Their magic naturally counters ours."

Dalton peered at the nerdy man. This was not his idea of what an evil wizard would look like. Voldemort, this guy *certainly* was not. "Jerry, if this coven you belong to is practicing black magic, why did you join it? I would never have thought of you as a practitioner of the dark arts."

"Well, it's not exactly like I joined, so to speak. I'm a Rubidoux cousin," he said and shrugged his skinny shoulders. "So, I was just sort of born into it."

"Lucky you." Dalton sighed.

"Are you telling me you've lived in this Parish all your life and never heard about the witches in the Black Bayou? I thought everybody here knew about us."

"My grandpa used to tell me and my sister stories about witches, ghosts, and the *loup-garou*, but we were kids. We thought they were just stories he told to scare us and keep us out of the swamp. Neither of us thought they were true."

"Yeah," he chuckled out, "we heard the same stories, but *we* grew up knowing they were true. The Rubidoux and DuBois families have been practicing witchcraft and selling charms and potions since coming down from Canada about three centuries ago. I can't believe you didn't know about it. Almost everybody in this Parish is related to a Rubidoux or a DuBois somehow, unless they're a recent transplant to the damned bayou. How long have your people been here?" Jerry asked.

Dalton ran a hand through his hair "I think my great grand-parents moved here from New Orleans after the Civil War."

"I'd have thought that would have been long enough to know about the magical families living here." Dalton watched the man mentally calculating. "That is over a hundred and fifty years ago."

"Yeah, I suppose. I'm at the Highgate apartments just around the corner up here," Dalton told him. "You can just drop me out front."

"Oh, yeah, sure thing." Jerry slowed the truck to make the turn into the apartment complex. "Better let me take you to your door, though. You still have a bit of blood on your face. We don't want to freak out the locals." He grinned.

Dalton's hand went involuntarily to his face, searching for crusty spots. "Apartment 1040, just up here. Thanks." Jerry parked his truck in an empty space outside Dalton's apartment. "Thanks for the ride and the information, Jerry.

"No problem. You really shouldn't have pissed Althea off. That woman has got a hell of a temper and never forgets a slight."

"Tell me about it." Dalton eased out of the truck, waved, and watched Jerry back up and drive away. He hurried into his modest one-bedroom apartment.

The patio door stood open, and his bed covers looked rumpled. Dalton remembered locking the doors before going to bed the night before. He found his phone on the nightstand to check the date, uncertain how long he'd been gone. Maybe Althea and her minions had drugged and held him for several days.

His fingers shook as he picked up the phone to see he'd only been gone overnight. He also saw three missed calls from Julia. He pulled up her number and hit send. Dalton eagerly awaited the sound of her sweet voice and gave a long sigh when she answered.

"Hi, Dalton. I've been calling since last night. Are you all right?"

"Hey, Jules. I just got home and saw your calls. I think I'm in trouble. Can you come by after work?"

"Sure, babe. What's happened?" Dalton heard the worry in her voice.

"Althea and her thugs paid me a visit during the night."

"I had an inkling that something went wrong last night."

"Your magical Spidey senses?" Dalton chuckled involuntarily.

"Something like that. It was the full moon. I knew if she were going to try and pull something, it would have been then. It's when our powers are at their fullest. What did she do?"

"Are you familiar with the *loup-garou*?" Dalton asked, and heard a sharp intake of breath on the other end of the phone.

"Oh my gods, she didn't."

Evidently, she did. "I woke up in a field this mornin' covered in blood. I don't know where it came from, but I think I chased something or somebody down last night."—his voice broke as he tried to contain a sob—"and killed it. I need your help, Jules if you're really a witch like you say you are."

"I'll be on my lunch break in five minutes. I'm taking the rest of the day off. I'll be right over." He heard her take a deep breath. "Don't worry, babe, we'll fix this."

The phone went silent, but Dalton breathed easy for the first time since waking up. Julia was coming, and she'd fix this *loup-garou* problem. Dalton shook his head at the thought. He couldn't believe he'd just thought those words. This *loup-garou* problem.

Dalton shook his head again and went into the bathroom to take a long, hot shower. His stomach turned violently when he saw the pink water collecting at his feet. Ripping aside the shower curtain, he jumped from the tub and bent over the toilet to empty his stomach. He heaved again when he saw what he'd thrown up. He'd filled his toilet stool with chunks of raw meat and torn skin with hair on it. It didn't look like human hair, and relief momentarily flooded through Dalton. It still sickened him that he'd chased, killed, and eaten an animal. Dalton heaved until light-headedness took him, and he slid down into the tub with the spray from the shower beating his aching muscles.

4

Julia rushed to clean up her workstation at the drive-thru window of the bank and made her excuses to her boss. She used her monthly female problem as the excuse for leaving mid-shift and ran to her car. After getting in and buckling up, Julia punched in the number for her brother, Bernard.

"Hi, sis, what's up?" Bernard asked. "You don't usually call me in the middle of the day. Is something wrong?"

"Your friend Althea has been at it again," Julia snapped. "That's what's wrong."

Bernard DuBois and Althea Rubidoux had been friends since high school. Julia knew Bernard had hoped to heal the rift between the two families, but neither coven wanted that. Too many harsh words and deeds had gone on between the two covens over the decades to be healed in one generation. Each had declared territories within the swamp for collecting herbs, and those boundaries were always in flux, with disputes erupting regularly. The last one, nearly a decade ago, had cost lives on both sides.

"What horrible infraction has she made now?" Bernard asked with a careless air. "Did she pick toadstools on your side of the line?"

23

"She's cast the *loup-garou* curse. That's something even *you* shouldn't excuse, Bernard," Julia fumed at her brother. "That curse has been forbidden to every coven for several centuries now. I need you to call a full coven meeting for tonight. I'm calling De la Croix in New Orleans. They need to know what's going on out here with that coven out on the island."

"Do you really want to get De la Croix involved? We've always handled our problems out here without getting the High Council involved, and I don't see why we should change that now."

"She's gone too far this time, Bernard. She cursed *my* man."

"Wasn't he *her* man first?" Bernard sneered. "The High Council isn't going to want to get called out here to the Bayou to referee a bitch-fight over a damned man."

"That's not really the point now, is it, Bernard? Althea used a curse banned by the High Council centuries ago because it puts all of us at risk. What if we can't perform the ritual to counter the curse before the next full moon and Dalton hurts somebody? The longer we wait to counter it, the harder it gets. If we can't counter it within a year, he'll be a *loup-garou* for the rest of his life, and we'll have no choice but to"—Julia's voice broke with a sob—"to kill him."

"Are you certain she actually did it and that she didn't just drug him and tell him she had done something when he came 'round? I wouldn't put that past her, but I don't think she'd actually break a Council Law like that one. They could sanction her and put her into the dungeons." Bernard sighed. "I don't think she'd risk that."

Councils governed the covens in each respective region of the world. A High Council oversaw those councils. The locations of the High Council moved every century. As of Samhain in 1999, the new High Council had been relocated to New Orleans and officiated over by the De la Croix Coven. Antoine De la Croix, the head of that powerful coven, was known to be a stern man who ran his coven with an iron fist. Now that he oversaw the

High Council, infractions of Council Laws were sure to be dealt with swiftly and severely.

"She probably thinks her daddy will buy off the High Council like he's bought off the local law all these years to keep her and her brothers out of jail."

"Don't get snippy now. Go check on your boy-toy and don't do anything we'll all regret before you confirm his condition. Talk to ya later." Her phone went silent.

Exasperated, Julia shut her phone off and turned into the Highgate Apartments, eager to see Dalton. If he turned out to be in the condition she suspected, De la Croix would be getting a call from her immediately. Julia jumped from her car, slammed the door without locking it, and rushed to Dalton's door. She found the door unlocked and went inside. Julia closed her eyes in the quiet living room. Residual power pulsed through her senses. She could feel the dark magic someone had used upon Dalton, and her anger rose. One person alone could not have channeled that much power safely. Althea must have used her entire coven to cast the *loup-garou* curse. If that was the case, the whole Rubidoux Coven could be sanctioned and even disbanded by the High Council.

Julia found Dalton snoring softly, sprawled naked across his bed. His head rested upon his arms, hugging the pillow tightly. Julia didn't want to disturb him, but she needed to get closer to gage the power of the spell used upon him. She knew Bernard's hope that Althea had simply pulled a mean prank wasn't the case. The Residual magic pulsed from his body like heat coming from red-hot metal. Julia didn't need more proof than this to know Althea and her coven had, indeed, cast the *loup-garou* curse upon Dalton La Pierre.

Time was now a critical factor. She only had until the next full moon to reverse the casting to keep Dalton from changing into the wolf-beast again. How could Althea do such a hideous thing to another human being?

Stepping from his room and pulling the door closed, Julia

took her phone from the pocket of her cardigan sweater and called her mother, the former High Priestess of the DuBois Coven.

"Hey, Sweetheart," her mother greeted in her usual cheery tone. "It's good to hear from you. How did last night go?" Julia, as the current High Priestess of their Coven, led the monthly Full Moon Ceremony, summoning the Goddess and asking for Blessings. "I just couldn't make it out there last night. My hip is going, and tramping out into the swamp would probably have kept me in my bed for days." Her mother chuckled, then took a breath. "I did a private ritual here with your dad. I hope you asked for Healing Blessings upon both of us. Your dad's heart is fluttering in and out of rhythm again."

"Mom, hang on a minute," Julia said to quiet her chattering mother. "This is important, Mom. I need you to call a coven meeting for tonight."

"What's happened, honey? Why do you want to call a full coven meeting when you just saw everyone last night?" her mother asked in a perplexed tone. "I hope it's not something trivial. You're a new leader. You can't just call meetings willy-nilly because you can."

"The Rubidoux Coven cast a *loup-garou* curse last night. They've broken Council Law and cursed a friend."

"The *loup-garou*? Are you certain?" Her mother's voice had turned deadly serious.

"Yes, Mom, I'm certain." Julia huffed. "I'm at his apartment now, and the place is fairly pulsing with Residual. It had to have been channeled by the entire coven for it to be this thick in the air."

"Oh my … Do you have valerian root at home? That will soothe the headache from the Residual."

"Yes, Mom, I have valerian," Julia assured her. "Now, please call everyone. We have to do the counter-curse before he can change with the next moon, I asked Bernard to call, but you know how he feels about Althea. He doesn't want to think she'd do it."

"Of course, sweetheart. Don't worry about that. I'll have everybody meet here. It'll be nice to have everybody around the fire-pit again," her mother said happily. Julia knew her mother had hated to give up her position as High Priestess, but her bad knees, bad hip, and husband's health problems had made it a necessity. Julia, trained practically from birth to assume the role someday, had stepped into her mother's position with ease and grace. Ruby DuBois still liked to host the coven, and Julia would not deny her that joy.

Julia slipped her phone back into her pocket but pulled it out again and ran through her contact list until she came to Antoine De la Croix. She hit send and waited through six rings. Julia wouldn't use voicemail to deliver this message to the head of the High Council.

"De la Croix here." A deep voice said into Julia's ear. "How may I help you?"

"Hello, sir," Julia said nervously. She'd met the imposing African American man at last fall's Witches' Ball in New Orleans, and Julia had to admit that he frightened her more than a little. "This is Julia DuBois from St. Elizabeth. I have something disturbing to relay."

"Yes?" he asked, inviting her to continue.

"The Rubidoux Coven has cast a *loup-garou* curse here."

"You are certain of this, young lady? A *loup-garou* casting is a serious charge to make against a neighboring coven. I know of the bad blood between your people out there."

"I'm not in the habit of making false claims," Julia said. "I'm standing in the home of the cursed man now, and the Residual is about to overwhelm me. I do not doubt the curse, and the man told me who admitted to cursing him. He had it directly from the mouth of Althea Rubidoux, High Priestess of the Rubidoux Coven."

"By the Gods," he said with irritation. "I've had calls about that woman from members of her own coven, but I thought they were simply women jealous of Althea's power and beauty." He paused. "She is quite beautiful, is she not?"

"Beauty on the outside does not translate to beauty on the inside, or so my mother has told me regularly."

"I know your lovely mother well." De La Croix said. "She's a smart woman and absolutely correct. I'm sure her Grimoire contains the necessary countermeasure for this unfortunate casting." He paused once more, and Julia heard him inhale. He must have been smoking one of those horrible cigars she'd seen between his fingers at last fall's gathering. "You are lucky to have her good counsel still. I hope she and your father are well."

"Yes, I'm lucky to have both my parents. They are well, but suffer from the general aches and pains of aging."

"Indeed," he said stoically. "I shall look into this matter of the *loup-garou* casting. If I find sufficient evidence, measures will be taken to rectify the situation of the Rubidoux Coven. I will not tolerate the breaking of High Council Law during my watch here. Thank you, Miss DuBois."

*I wonder what constitutes sufficient evidence. Maybe I should wait and sit Dalton in De la Croix's living room for the next full moon. And why does everybody keep asking me if I'm certain? Of course, I'm certain. I've been trained to sense magic all my damned life. My own mother asked, and she's the one who taught me.*

Julia heard Dalton's bedroom door open, and then the sound of him relieving himself in the bathroom. He trudged out into the living room naked and looking forlorn.

"Hey, Jules." Dalton bent and kissed Julia on the forehead. "I thought I heard your voice. What time is it? How long did I sleep?" He stretched his lean, muscular body.

"It's a little past two. I've been here for a while." Julia slipped her phone back into her pocket. "I didn't want to wake you." She sat on the couch beside Dalton and took his hand. The pulsing Residual from the spell radiated from his body. Julia could hardly stand to touch him. Pain sparked behind her eyes, and she wished she had some of the valerian root here. "I've been making some calls, and I've arranged for a full coven meeting tonight at my mom and dad's place. I think you should come with me so everyone can see what's been done to you."

Dalton screwed up his face in confusion. "What do you mean by 'see what's been done to me'?" Horror suddenly etched itself on Dalton's handsome face. "Is the moon still full? Will I turn into that thing again tonight?"

"No, it will only happen on the actual night of the monthly full moon." Julia squeezed his hand. "We, who've been trained, can feel the magic that's been used on you." She took a deep breath before continuing to let her words sink in. "I need to take you to the meeting so there will be no doubt amongst my coven members that the entire Rubidoux Coven had to be involved in channeling that spell."

"I still don't understand what you mean by '*y'all can feel the magic.*'"

"We who practice magic develop a sensitivity to it." Julia lay her head back on the couch to collect her thoughts. "Think of magic as vibrations. Right now, your body is sending out Residual vibrations that I can feel. Some in the coven won't be that sensitive, but the ones I need to convince are. Get dressed," Julia said with an impish grin. "I'm taking you home to meet the family."

## 5

Nervous did not begin to explain how Dalton felt as they turned into the drive of the DuBois family home. To him, the place looked like Tara from *Gone with the Wind*. Massive white columns held up a balcony edged with wrought-iron railings. The red brick construction of the antebellum period mansion screamed old money and a lot of it. Still, Julia had to be one of the most down-to-earth people Dalton had ever met, unlike the pretentious Althea Rubidoux, who only wore designer clothing and drove a Benz.

Several cars lined the circular drive paved with the same red brick as the house. Julia drove around to the back of the property, where someone had converted the old coach house into the family's garage. She parked her unpretentious PT Cruiser next to another car sitting in front of white garage doors.

"Looks like my brother Bernard and his wife are here already," Julia said, nodding toward the silver Lexus. "Watch what you say about Althea in front of him. They've been close for years."

"How close?" Dalton asked with a raised eyebrow.

Julia shrugged her shoulders as she opened the door of her electric blue PT Cruiser. "I don't know if they had that kind of friendship, but I know they still talk. She must have really bent his ear about us, though. He knew all about it, and I haven't mentioned you to the family yet."

Dalton didn't know how to take that. He'd been seeing Julia for more than a month and thought they had clicked on more than one level, yet she hadn't brought him up to her family. He hadn't brought her up to his family, either, but he seldom talked to his parents anymore. He and his sister, Marsha, had been in a car accident five years earlier, and Marsha died in the accident. His parents blamed him for her death and had all but disowned him after the funeral.

Julia led him to a white picket gate and opened it. Dalton could hear conversation and laughter coming from beyond and saw the flickering glow of an open fire. The scent of wood smoke stung his nose and hung in the heavy, humid night air. They walked side-by-side to a patio where a dozen or more couples sat around a blazing fire pit.

"Hey, everybody," Julia greeted the group. "This is Dalton La Pierre." She pushed him toward them and whispered, "Shake all their hands, babe."

The first person they came to was a thin woman in her sixties with curly salt-and-pepper hair. Dalton could not mistake her resemblance to Julia. Dalton took the woman's outstretched hand, and her reaction stunned him. She threw her head back, and her knees gave way from beneath her. Dalton caught Julia's mother's slight body in his strong arms. Several men jumped up to take her from Dalton.

As soon as Dalton released her, she began to come around. "Ben," she gasped, taking her frail husband's hand, "don't you dare touch that boy. The Residual would stop your heart for sure."

"I'm sorry, Mom. I had no idea it was going to affect you that way." Julia knelt by her mother, who now sat in one of the many white Adirondack chairs surrounding the fire pit. "I just wanted you to know I wasn't crying wolf." Julia touched Dalton's shoulder. "No pun intended, sweetheart."

He looked back at her, confused, and then gave her a weak smile. "Oh, yeah, right."

Others in the group walked up to Dalton and very gently touched him on this back, shoulders, or arms. Some took his hand but released it quickly.

"She certainly did a number on you," said a tall red-headed man, wearing Dockers and a crisp cotton short-sleeved shirt that buttoned down the front. "You really shouldn't have fucked around on Althea Rubidoux, even if it *was* with my sister. I'm Bernard DuBois."

Dalton eyed the man wearily before taking his hand. "So I've been told by more than one person today."

"Can I get you a beer or something, buddy?" Bernard asked.

"Yeah, sure, a beer would be great."

"You want one too, Sis?"

"Yes, please," Julia replied, still kneeling by her mother, who sipped a Pepsi from a can. Julia stood up straight, gathered herself before the group, and took Dalton's hand. "Althea and the Rubidoux Coven have used the *loup-garou* curse on this man. We don't have much time to find everything we need for the counter-curse." Julia touched her mother's shoulder. "You have that in your Grimoire, don't you? If you don't, I can get it from De la Croix."

Dalton heard sharp intakes of breath in the group at the mention of the High Council leader's name.

"Yes, of course I have it, sweetheart." The woman rested her Pepsi can on the broad arm of the chair. "I should have handed my Grimoire down to you when I stepped aside. That book has been handed down from Priestess to Priestess in our family for centuries. Many of the oldest texts are written in Old French and Latin. They've been translated and scribbled out in English or modern French. The *loup-garou* and its counter are in there. Nobody has had to use the counter in the centuries since the

Banning. I can't believe that girl would take the chance of crossing De la Croix." Ruby DuBois shook her head and stood on shaky legs. "He's liable to put her in the dungeons or possibly even have her executed." Dalton watched Julia and her mother walk into the big house through multi-paned French doors.

He couldn't believe what he was hearing. The woman had actually used the words dungeons and executed. He shook his head and sipped his beer, sitting in one of the deep-seated lawn chairs.

Bernard tapped Dalton's shoulder. "She didn't actually call De la Croix, did she?" He looked uncomfortable, and his broad smile had faded to a thin line.

"I have no idea," Dalton said, shrugging his shoulder. "Jules was on the phone when I woke up, but I don't know who she was talking to."

"If she pulls De la Croix into this mess, we're all in the shit." Bernard chugged his beer.

"Why?" Dalton asked. "Isn't he the big Kahuna over all of you down here? Wouldn't he be the one she'd go to?"

"We tend to our own business out here in the bayou," Bernard snapped. "We don't want any big-city Voodoo bastard out here messing in our shit. If Althea and her coven have broken Council Law, we'll deal with them in our own way."

"Bernard," his father interrupted, "it's your sister's place as the Mother of this coven to make the critical decisions, and you have no place bad-mouthing her about it." The older man took a drink of his beer and glared at his son. "Keep your opinions to yourself. I won't hear it in my home."

"Sure, Dad," Bernard whined, "she can bring De la Croix and the damned High Council down on top of our heads, and we're just supposed to sit here and say nothing like good little followers."

"I'll deal with De la Croix." They all jumped at Julia's loud, clear voice from behind them. "It was my call to make, and I made it. Althea Rubidoux and her coven have gone too far this

33

time. We've allowed them to get away with far too much over the years." Dalton could smell the irritation radiating from her and turned to see Julia carrying a large leather-bound book with a strap and brass lock securing it.

Julia's mother stood by her daughter wearing a smug look. "I would not have turned the care of this Coven over to my daughter if I'd had any doubts about her ability to lead it. If any of you," she stared directly at her son as she took a chain from about her neck with a delicate key dangling from it and transferred it to the neck of her daughter, "have anything to say about it, come to me. If you doubt Julia's abilities, then you doubt mine and my judgment. I now transfer to her, Julia DuBois, my total control of this coven with all my confidence in her abilities to lead. "

"Mother, I don't doubt either of you," Bernard said, looking like a little boy who'd just been caught with his hand in the cookie jar, "I simply think we should keep the High Council out of our shit down here. We've been governing ourselves for hundreds of years. Why should that change now with this one correctable infraction of the Laws?"

"Son, casting a *loup-garou* is far from being a simple infraction. There is a good reason they banned it in the first place," Ruby said as she returned to her chair. "People think witches and werewolves are simply made up to scare children. What do you think would happen to us if people knew that magic really existed?" She took a deep breath and a sip of her Pepsi. "The governments would try to round us up and use us as weapons. Not to mention what the religious fanatics would do to us. The Burning Times could easily return, and where could we run now? There are no more New Worlds for us to escape to."

Julia patted her mother's shoulder. "Don't fret over it, Mom." She looked out over the flames in the fire pit to address the others sitting there. "What I called this meeting for is to organize the counter-curse ritual to reverse Dalton's condition." Julia held up the weighty tome she now carried. "I'm going to study the

DuBois Grimoire tonight and make a list of the herbs and items we're going to need. Mother has read it, and it's a very complicated one requiring some obscure ingredients." Julia glanced around the circle. "Mary, you and Hal know the bayou like the backs of your hands. If I give you a list of herbs we're going to need, can you put together a hunting party to find them?"

A rotund woman wearing a tight black t-shirt stood along with a man almost as large. Dalton thought they must be the ones in town keeping the Sonic in business.

"Sure, Julia, no problem," said the woman. "Just email me the list and we'll get right on it. Peggy and Tom know where most of the medicinals grow out there, as well. They'll be my team." She nodded to a man with long white hair and a beard like one of the Duck Commanders, sitting with a thin blonde next to him. They nodded and agreed to help.

"We only have until the next Moon to accomplish this." Julia went to stand behind Dalton. She clenched his shoulder in her hands. "This man did nothing but decide to love me rather than Althea Rubidoux." She bent and kissed the top of Dalton's head. "No man deserves the *loup-garou*, and especially not this one. I say we meet here every week to discuss our progress. Is that all right with you, Mom?"

"Of course, it is, sweetheart," Ruby DuBois said with a broad smile. "Why don't we make it an hour earlier next week and have a potluck. Ben and I will supply meat to grill for those of you who still eat it, and everyone with last names beginning with A through M bring main courses. Those of you with N through Z bring deserts."

With the next week's meeting planned and their course set, the DuBois Coven began to disperse, leaving Dalton and Julia sitting with her parents, her brother, and his cute little blonde wife, Terry. Dalton remembered Terry from school. She'd been a year ahead of him and a cheerleader.

"Well, Dalton," Terry said, laying a delicate hand carefully on his arm, "I guess all of this must seem pretty out there to you.

Witches, werewolves, and the like." She gave him a tiny smile. "Or had you already heard about the witches of the Black Bayou? I think just about everyone out here has."

"My grandpa used to tell me and my sister tales about witches, ghosts, and the *loup-garou*," Dalton said as he absently slapped at a mosquito. "We just thought they were scary stories to keep us out of the swamp."

"So did I until my aunt Lilly got sick. The doctors told her she only had months to live. She had a seriously diseased liver from Hep-C," Terry explained. "I had just started datin' Bernard, and he saw how upset my mama and I were. He talked to his parents about it and told me to get some hair from my aunt's brush and a photo of her. He picked me up one night and told me to bring those things with me."

Terry rubbed Dalton's forearm as she spoke quietly. "He took me out to the place where they have their altar and gave me a robe to wear. Ruby cast the Circle with her Athame," she smiled when Dalton looked confused. "It's a ritual dagger with a black handle," Terry explained. "Then she lit incense in an iron cauldron. Ruby called down the Goddess, passed around my aunt's picture for everyone to see, and then put it into the cauldron with the hair. As the smoke rose into the air, the whole group chanted healing chants." Terry took a sip of the beer she'd been holding. "I don't know how, but I found myself chanting along even though I didn't know the words. They just came to me somehow."

"Did your aunt get better?" Dalton asked skeptically.

"She got the call from the transplant clinic the very next day that a liver had become available. It really was a miracle," Terry said wide-eyed. "Aunt Lily has a very rare blood type, and the people at the clinic had told her the likelihood of finding a match was like a million to one. That ritual worked. I swear it did. Aunt Lily had maybe days left, and after that ritual, a longshot liver became available because a guy with the right blood type got killed in a car accident? That was magic, and I was a part of it. After that, I joined the Circle with Bernard."

"How long have you two been together now?" Dalton asked before finishing his own beer.

"It'll be ten years next month," she sighed out. "Ten great years, two great kids, a dog, and two not so great cats. It's been a good life." Terry saw Bernard moving toward the gate and rose. She hugged Dalton. "Don't worry, hun. We'll take care of this shit." She gave him a quick peck on the cheek and smiled sheepishly. "And welcome to the family."

Dalton watched Terry skip off to join her husband and disappear through the gate. Julia joined him, taking the chair next to his. "What did you and Terry have your heads together for over here?"

"She was just telling me about how she joined your family and how she learned about the witch stuff with Bernard."

Julia smiled. "Terry's been a good addition to our Circle. She has a natural empathic ability to pick up on things. She's open-minded and attuned to the natural forces around her. Most people these days aren't."

Dalton yawned, nodding his head in agreement. "I'd probably be one of those who aren't."

"You never know," Julia said, smiling. She stretched herself over to kiss his mouth. "You're very attuned to me. I've sensed something in you since we first met. I'm sure that skank, Althea, did as well, and it's why she was so keen to hang onto you."

"Do I sense a hint of jealousy in you, daughter?" Ruby said from behind them. "You two can stay and enjoy the fire, but I need to get your father to bed."

"No, we're going, too, Mom. Dalton is beat, as you might imagine." Julia stood to follow her parents into the house to get her purse.

Dalton sat staring into the dying flames. As he peered into them, a face began to materialize before his eyes. Althea Rubidoux's face glared back at him. Dalton wanted to run, but he couldn't move, transfixed by the smoldering eyes of his former lover.

"You are mine, Dalton La Pierre. With that curse, you are mine forever." Dalton heard Althea's hideous laughter. Ice ran through his veins, and he began to shiver in the warm damp Louisiana night.

"I think not, bitch," Julia said before dousing the flames with the remainder of a beer.

"You saw that?" Dalton stammered.

"Yes," she said and took Dalton's cold, shaking hand. "Her curse has linked the two of you somehow. I'll talk to my mom about it in the morning and study the Grimoire to see if there's some way to break the connection. It's very possible," Julia told him, "that she can only use fire or still water to enable the connection. I've heard of that.

Julia pulled him to his feet.

"Come on, babe, let's get you home so that you can get some sleep."

## 6

They drove in silence back to Julia's cottage. Neither wanted to tempt fate by returning to Dalton's apartment, where Althea and her people had abducted him the night before. Dalton found Julia's little clapboard house charming. It had probably been built in the nineteenth century by one of the free persons of color who populated St. Elizabeth back then.

Tall windows graced the walls, and the floors had never been covered with wall-to-wall carpeting or hideous linoleum. The two bedrooms, while roomy, did not have closets. When the house had been built, people used free-standing wardrobes in which to hang their clothes. Dalton had seen some very ornate ones in antique stores, and Julia had one in each bedroom. The only bathroom in the little house had been built off the kitchen where an open porch had once been. Someone had added the bathroom sometime in the early twentieth century and never dug a proper foundation to support the outside walls and fixtures in the room.

When Dalton had asked Julia why she'd bought such a dated old house, the perky little redhead had told him it was for that very reason.

"I love this house. It has the character of the old owners,"

Julia said, passing him a beer to go with his popcorn as they'd watched a black and white rerun of the movie *Rebecca*. "I know the spirits of the previous owners are happy with what I've done with the place."

"Spirits?" Dalton asked, wide-eyed. "You mean, like, ghosts?"

"I'm not going to do any more structural work on the house after the utility room is enclosed. It riles the spirits attached to the house to change it too much." Julia took a long drink of her beer. "Don't you ever watch Ghost Hunters or any of those shows?"

"You mean that shit's all true and not just made up for television?"

"I don't see why it wouldn't be," she'd said. "They seem to have plenty of evidence that it is, and I know of local people who can see and talk to spirits, so it must be true to some extent."

Dalton shrugged. "I suppose you have a point, but why would ghosts care if you remodel the house?"

"The theory is that they don't like living people screwing with their shit." Julia stuffed a handful of the white kernels into her mouth. "I guess if you'd been living in the same place for a couple of hundred years, you wouldn't want some strangers coming in and mucking about with it."

"They get pissed if you're making it better?"

"Better than what? They had no use for flush toilets or walk-in closets and have no use for them now. It's simply better to leave well enough alone. I think it looks great just the way it is."

Julia had replaced worn and broken storm-shutters, had the roof fixed, and new shingles installed but refused to change anything more. Embossed tin tiles covered the ceilings that Julia had painted, and she'd stripped and refinished the old cypress floors, bringing out rich brown and orange hues in the wood. The first time Julia had built a fire in the fireplace, smoke billowed into the living room. A family of raccoons had taken up residence in the chimney at some point while the house stood empty and packed it solid with their nesting material.

In the three years since buying it, she'd made it her own, decorating with antiques from the period the house had been built during and furnishing it with modern-day reproductions. This house was nothing like the grand DuBois mansion she'd grown up in, but Julia appreciated the simplicity of the small cottage. She knew it irked her parents and brother that she lived in a house built by former slaves, while the DuBois mansion was a house fit for the masters.

Gardening was a hobby of Julia's, too, and she had flowers blooming year-round on the property. Rare and hard to acquire herbs grew in her garden out back, along with fresh vegetables. Fruit trees dotted the yard, shaded by magnificent old pecan trees.

Julia was confident the spirits living around the property were happy with her as a tenant of their home. She burned frankincense, myrrh, and copal regularly to appease them as well as to keep the mustiness of the damp Louisiana bayou at bay.

She led Dalton to the bedroom she'd claimed for herself. Both rooms measured the same, but this one was the closest to the only bathroom. If she'd taken the other, she'd have had to maneuver through the living room and the kitchen to use the toilet at night. Julia rarely had overnight guests in the other bedroom, so this was the wisest choice.

"Come on, babe, let's get you to bed. You can run to your apartment tomorrow and pick up whatever you need."

"Are you kidnapping me, Jules? Is this just a ruse to move me into your house and your bed," Dalton teased.

"I leave the kidnapping up to Althea," Julia retorted and threw a pillow at him. "You'd better be nice, or I'll take the *loup-garou* off and replace it with the notorious frog spell. You could spend the rest of your days down by the river dodging gators and giggers."

"You're kidding me, right? There's not really a frog spell. Is there?" Dalton asked with a straight face.

"Don't give me shit, and you'll never have to find out." Julia stripped off her t-shirt and pulled down her jeans. She watched Dalton doing the same. "I'm sorry, Dalton. I shouldn't be kidding you about that tonight. You must be a wreck."

"I grew up here, Jules, and I must be the only person in the entire damned Parish who never believed any of the spooky stories about the supernatural goings-on out here." Dalton shook his head and plopped down upon the soft pillow-top mattress.

"Most parents teach their children not to believe. They've turned *my* reality into a world of make-believe, and that's actually all right. Like my mom said, if people knew the truth about what we are and what we can do, we could all be in grave danger. So long as it remains in the world of fiction and teen angst television, we're safe." Julia turned off the light on her bedside table. "It would be like the vampires on *Trueblood*. If real witches came out of the shadows, there could be hell to pay."

"Wait a minute," Dalton gasped as he bolted upright in the bed. "*Are* there actually vampires out there? Is New Orleans really full of blood-sucking monsters?"

"Is it really so impossible to believe now? You didn't believe in witches or werewolves until today." Julia rolled and cupped his face in the darkness. "No, my love, New Orleans is not rife with vampires.," she said with a soft giggle, "and neither is Bon Temps. That curse was forbidden, as well."

Dalton fell back onto his pillow. "Are you fucking with my head again? Witches can make vampires, too?"

"Did you ever see that old soap opera from the sixties called *Dark Shadows*? It was about a man who'd been cursed by a witch and turned into a vampire. That was absolutely correct. A member of a New England coven feared that the New Agers just coming into being back then were going to give us all away.

"He pitched the idea for the supernatural soap opera to daytime television. They bought it, and the show became very popular." Julia yawned and stretched. "Because it was on televi-sion, the skeptics prevailed. Witches with magical powers, vampires, and werewolves couldn't possibly be real. It was all just make-believe."

"Wow," Dalton said. "I think I need to go to sleep now. I don't believe I can take any more supernatural revelations in one day."

Julia felt him roll over, but a few minutes later, he rolled again. Dalton tossed and turned for a while before falling asleep, and she couldn't blame him. The poor guy had just found out that he'd been changed into a werewolf and had been sleeping with two different witches. All the boogie men from his child-hood were coming to life around him.

Once Julia heard his even breathing and a few soft snores, she crept out of bed and went into the living room where the DuBois Grimoire set upon her coffee table. As a child, Julia remembered her mother reading the big book and how she had begged to look at it, but her mother had refused, promising her that one day the book would be hers and then she could study it as much as she liked.

When her mother had stepped down as High Priestess and turned things over to her, Julia had been surprised to find the book missing from the wooden chest that contained the other ritual items of the DuBois Circle. She supposed her mother needed to hang onto that one thing for a while longer to remind her of what she'd been for so many years. Holding the big book on her lap now, Julia thought she understood. The book's rich leather, bound in brass, was substantial. The name DuBois sten-ciled in gold leaf upon the cover gave Julia a great sense of pride.

She took the tiny brass key suspended on a gold chain from around her neck and inserted it into the lock on the front of the massive tome. The lock released, and Julia opened the big book. Upon the first page in an ornate script read Grimoire DuBois. The pages were not paper, but parchment made from specially treated goatskin. Julia ran her fingers over the page and wondered at the hundreds of other fingers that had done the same thing over the ages. The next few pages held the names of those women and the years they'd taken possession of the Grimoire.

Julia stared down at the first name and year written there; Juliette DuBois 1215. On the line below her mother's name, she would pen Julia DuBois and the year. This book had passed through the hands of DuBois witches for eight hundred years. She couldn't wait to study the knowledge contained within. The book had spent four hundred years in France before the Revolution, and the Inquisition had forced the family to flee to the New World. Even there, they'd faced religious persecution and fled north into the wild Canadian provinces from the Puritan Colonies.

In less than a hundred years, the family had joined other French families who'd traveled down the Mississippi River in small boats, rafts, and canoes until they reached southern Louisiana. Some had settled in and around New Orleans, but others had ventured farther out into the wilds of the swampy bayous, hoping to find a place to live where they could practice their ancient faith in peace.

The DuBois and the Rubidoux found their sanctuary around the Black Bayou. They had been there for over three hundred years. They'd weathered the American Revolution and the Civil War. Wars on foreign soil had never mattered to them, and no DuBois man or boy had ever been drafted. A few had volunteered during the First and Second World Wars because they felt a duty to France. The DuBois did not dabble in politics. They paid their property taxes and reluctantly, income tax. Wards had been set around their property to keep away unwanted guests like tax collectors, Revenue Agents, and Jehovah's Witnesses.

Julia turned the stiff pages decorated with brightly painted floral borders like those of medieval scrolls. Lines of neat script covered the space in the center. Julia peered closely at the text written in Old French and Latin. Beneath most lines were penciled translations into modern English.

Most of the handwriting she didn't know, but in other places, Julia recognized the neat hands of her grandmother and mother. They had scribbled in margins here and there. It looked like the old cookbook her mother had that had been passed down for generations with redactions scribbled in the margins, telling the modern cook the proper measurement of a pinch or a goodly portion. Julia had often wondered how those old cooks had ended up with anything edible.

When dealing with magical recipes, the proper measurements were essential to a successful outcome. Julia shook her head, wondering how many people had died of poisoning because of improper measurements of ingredients. Too large a pinch of belladonna for dropsy would end up in the patient dropping permanently.

As Julia turned the pages, she noticed that the illuminations around the texts usually had something to do with the spell within the margins. She carefully turned the pages until she found one with the snarling visage of a wolf in the corners. In bold letters, she recognized *Loup-garou*.

This was what she had been searching for. Across the bottom of the page was inked in a bold script: Banned by High Council 1251. Julia turned to the next page to find the counter-curse. She had no idea who had written the original or when, but the modern script gave an exact translation. In her notebook, she meticulously wrote the list of necessary ingredients. Wolf's bane had not surprised her, but the nectar of honeysuckle certainly had. The lengthy list of ingredients called for a solution of silver as well. She grinned to herself, thinking the movies hadn't gotten it completely wrong, after all. Two or three of the ingredients she did not recognize, but she was sure her botanist friends would. She smiled to herself when she read the glands of a certain tree-frog would be needed. She would undoubtedly have to tease Dalton with that.

In the margins, Julia took note that the spell had to take place at a specific point during the moon's cycle across the night sky. This was marked with bold exclamation points, meaning it must be crucial to the ritual.

She bit her lip and wondered how many witches had missed the critical point and were killed when the victim they were trying to save changed mid-spell. Julia made the sign of the pentagram over her breast and prayed to the Goddesses for her protection and guidance. She double-checked her notes and double-checked again until she was sure she had everything. Then she popped open her laptop and emailed the list to Mary and Hal. She'd leave that in their capable hands.

While she had her laptop open, Julia looked up some of the plants she hadn't recognized. One was a cousin to the mistletoe plant, and another was an obscure fungus. She hoped they could be found in the swamps around the bayou and not something that could only be found in France or Eastern Europe. She set aside her laptop and turned a few more pages of the Grimoire. Then she found a fountain pen on her desk drawer and, in a neat script, inscribed her name and the year at the bottom of the long list of DuBois witches.

# 7

Savage dreams plagued Dalton's nights. He discussed it with Julia, questioning her about whether or not she thought they were actual memories of his night as a *loup-garou* or simply nightmares caused by his stress over the entire situation.

"I can't honestly say, babe, but I wouldn't put it past Althea to be sending you nightmares. She has created a psychic bond between the two of you and could easily be putting nightmares into your head."

"Well, isn't that just great," Dalton growled. "I don't know what I ever saw in that bitch."

"Your cock," Julia laughed. "You saw your big hard cock *in* her." She swatted his wet naked behind as he stepped out of the shower.

"I have one of those for you now if you want it." He held his stiff cock in his hand, stroking it slowly. Julia sat on the toilet, shaving her shapely legs, and Dalton wanted nothing more than to spread them apart and shove himself inside her. They hadn't had sex once since his moving into the little cottage. Maybe Julia didn't want to have sex with a wolf-man?

"I can certainly understand if you don't want to be with me

until we get this thing taken off me. I guess you probably think I'm gross now or something." His cock throbbed in his hand, and the scent of her filling his nostrils was driving him crazy with need and desire.

"Where the hell is that coming from?" Julia reached out and took his hand. "You're the sweetest, sexiest *man* I've ever known." She pulled him closer to where she sat and set the razor onto the vanity. "Being cursed doesn't change that in any way." Julia took his erection into her hand and stroked it. She pulled him closer until the organ stood only inches from her soft, glistening lips. Her mouth touched him, and Dalton shivered. The redhead's tongue lapped at the underside of the pulsing head, and he moaned with pleasure.

"Oh, Jules, that feels so good." Julia parted her soft pink lips and took his cock into her hot, wet mouth. Dalton threaded his fingers into her red curls and pushed and pulled her head as his cock slid in and out of her mouth. She couldn't take all of him and used her hand to slide in unison with her tight lips. "I'm not gonna last long this morning, and that feels so damned good," Dalton panted. Her other hand found his balls and gently squeezed them. Dalton's senses flared.

He could smell her musky sex wafting up from where she sat with her legs open. It excited him, and he wanted more than just her mouth. Dalton tried to pull back, but Julia refused to let go of his erection. It was just as well because his throbbing cock didn't want to leave her beautiful mouth. He was only seconds from exploding when he pushed her head onto his erection. "Good God, woman, here it comes." He let out a guttural howl as his release burst into Julia's mouth. He felt her swallow before his wilted cock slipped from between her lips, which made a shiver run through his body. Julia looked up at him, smiling sheepishly.

"All better now?" She wrapped her arms around his waist. "You're the man of my dreams, Dalton, and don't you ever think otherwise. We're going to counter this damned curse, and everything will be fine. You'll see. Now let me up, or I'm going to be late for work."

He pulled her to her feet and kissed her passionately. "You're the best, Jules."

"I like you too," she quipped as she slipped from the bathroom to the bedroom. "Don't forget, we have the meeting at my mom's tomorrow night."

"How could I possibly forget? My future depends on it." He pulled underwear and socks from the drawer in her dresser that she'd emptied for him. Dalton pulled on the white briefs and a t-shirt, then put on his jeans and buckled his belt. Sitting on the edge of the bed, he pulled on white socks, followed by steel-toed work boots. "I won't forget, Jules. What are we taking as our offering to the potluck?"

"When I get home tonight, I'm going to make a fruit salad and a tray of deviled eggs. They're my dad's favorite, and I usually make them for him when we have these things."

"Yummy. They're my favorite too." Dalton kissed Julia again and left her house in better spirits.

On his way to his garage, he drove through the McDonalds to pick up a black coffee and a sausage muffin. He glanced up to see Althea's black Mercedes sitting in the parking lot and, to his surprise, he saw Bernard DuBois's silver Lexus parked a few spaces down. Dalton drove slowly past the wide window of the fast-food restaurant, and he could clearly see the couple sitting together, holding hands across the little table. Surely Bernard wasn't swapping spit with Althea Rubidoux when all of this was going on. Unusual anger and rage consumed him.

Dalton drove across the street and parked his truck in the Auto Zone lot. He drank his coffee and ate his muffin while watching for Althea and Bernard to leave and go to their cars. It wasn't long before the couple walked out, holding hands. When they got to Althea's car, Dalton watched as Bernard took the tall woman into his arms and kissed her.

It infuriated Dalton that they didn't seem to care who might see them together. St. Elizabeth wasn't a big town, the population barely topping three thousand, and everybody knew everybody. Cars passing on the street had a clear view of the couple, and Dalton wondered if this affair was a hot topic on the gossip grapevine already. With his anger mounting, Dalton also wondered how Bernard could do this to a sweet woman like Terry. Dalton took a deep breath to clear his head of the rage building inside him. He wanted to chase Bernard down and chew his head off.

He waited until their cars left the parking lot before backing out and driving on to his Garage and Wrecker Service. In his fury, Dalton considered calling Julia to tell her what he'd witnessed but decided against it. He didn't want to upset her at work. He didn't want to upset her at all, but he thought she needed to know that her deceitful brother was evidently sleeping with the enemy.

His day was fraught with fits of rage and anger. Dalton found himself tossing tools across the garage and cussing at inanimate objects for no reason. He ignored radio calls and kicked the tires of his wrecker. When five-o-clock finally rolled around, he locked up and drove back to Julia's. His inexplicable rage had cooled, but he intended to tell Julia about what he'd seen as soon as he saw her.

Dalton smelled chicken frying when he walked through the door, and his mouth began to water. He'd skipped lunch because his anger at Bernard had ruined his appetite. In the kitchen, Julia stood over the range turning chicken in an iron skillet. Other pots steamed upon burners. It looked as though she was going all out in the kitchen for him tonight.

"Hey, Jules. It smells great in here." He kissed her cheek and patted her behind.

"Since I was going to do the eggs," she said and nodded to one of the boiling pots, "I thought I'd go ahead and cook something. I get tired of pizza and burgers all the time." Julia turned away from the stove, stretched up on her tiptoes, and kissed Dalton. "How was your day?"

"Not good." he took off his cap and ran his greasy fingers through his sweaty curls.

"Why? I thought I started it off good for you," Julia said and gave him an impish grin.

"You did, and I loved it, but ..." he sat in one of the ladder-back chairs placed along the farm table and took a deep breath. "But I saw something that made me really angry, and I couldn't seem to shake it all day."

"What did you see?" Julia turned off the burner under the popping chicken. She then hefted a steaming pot from the stove and poured the contents into a colander in the deep farm sink. "What got you so upset that it stayed with you all day? Must have been pretty bad."

"You're not gonna like it."

"What?" she asked and turned to face him with her brow furrowed in concern.

Dalton cleared his throat, collecting his thoughts. "I went through the drive up for coffee at McDonald's this morning, and I saw Althea's car in the parking lot."

She sighed with relief. "Is that all?"

"No, it's not all. Your brother's car was sitting next to it."

"I told you they were friends from school. They get together from time to time for coffee or lunch." Julia took milk and butter out from the refrigerator.

"They were a little more than friendly, Jules. They were sitting together in the middle of McDonald's holding hands like a couple of high school sweethearts at lunch hour," Dalton told her. "It was disgusting to see them together like that, and pissed me off.

"What? How could you tell from the truck? That glass is tinted. I can hardly see through it."

"I could see them as clear as day. They were holding hands on top of the table." Dalton cleared his throat again before continuing. "I drove across to the Auto Zone to eat my muffin, and I saw them come out together, holding hands and looking all lovey-dovey." He paused again. "Then Bernard kissed her, and it wasn't a friendly peck on the cheek. He grabbed her up in his arms and laid one on her good right there in the parking-lot where anyone passing could see."

The simmering rage took hold of Dalton once more. "I can't believe he'd do that to Terry. She told me the other night that their marriage is good, and she sounded so happy and bragged about their ten years together. And then he's out smooching it up with Althea in a parking lot for everyone in town to see. It just pissed me off."

Julia stood open-mouthed with the potato masher gripped white-knuckled in her hand, staring at Dalton. "You must have been mistaken, babe. With everything going on, I'm certain Bernard wouldn't be consorting with Althea like *that*."

"I didn't want to upset you, Jules, but I thought you should know." Dalton stood up and went to Julia, who looked as though someone had just punched her in the gut. "I'm sorry."

He put his arms around her, but Julia shook him off, grabbed her phone from the counter, and furiously punched in a number. Julia put the phone to her ear.

"Hey, Terry. How are things?" Dalton listened as Julia tried to sound cheery. "Yeah, the eggs are boiling now. You know I can't disappoint Dad." Julia paused. "I've been trying to get hold of Bernard, but he's not picking up. Yeah? Where? No, he didn't mention it. No, it's nothing important. I'll talk to him tomorrow. OK, sweetie, bye."

Julia dropped the phone back onto the counter with a sullen look. "It seems my dear brother has been in New Orleans on business for the past *two* days and won't be back until tomorrow. You're certain it was Bernard?"

"Yep. I saw him *and* his car. He wasn't in New Orleans at seven this morning."

Julia threw a considerable dollop of butter and sloshed milk from the plastic jug into her pan before taking her anger out on the potatoes with the masher. "I'm going to kick his sorry ass when I see him. He's got a wife and two kids at home. What the hell does he think he's doing with that skanky bitch?"

## 8

J ulia couldn't rest easy that night, tossing and turning. Around three, she finally gave up on sleep and went into the living room to study the Grimoire. She'd hoped it would take her mind off her brother, but it hadn't, and she went to work the next morning bleary-eyed with dark circles beneath her lashes. Her day, it seemed, dragged on forever.

She hoped to get in a nap before going to her parents', but her cash drawer hadn't balanced, and she had to stay over for nearly an hour and a half to find the ten-dollar discrepancy.

When Julia arrived home, she was happy to see Dalton's truck parked in the drive. She pulled up beside it and got out. The scent of the honeysuckle that twined through the rusty mesh wire of the old back fence filled Julia's nose and rejuvenated her spirits for the night to come.

Inside, Dalton had lit some of her favorite incense, and the house smelled of frankincense and sandalwood. The combination settled the nerves and cleared negativity. Julia's appreciation of the man, who'd moved into the house with her heightened tenfold. Although he'd been thrown into this reality so harshly, she saw Dalton embracing it. He listened to her as she explained magical principles and how they bent the laws of physics and science. He didn't understand it yet, but his open-mindedness thrilled her. Julia could picture a future with this man and perhaps a place in the DuBois Coven's monthly circle.

"Thanks for the incense, babe. That was sweet," Julia said when she saw him standing at the counter in the kitchen. He turned to face her, and Julia screamed in terror. His face was contorted into the snarling visage of a *loup-garou*. He raised his hands, and the hairy fingers were tipped with savage, hooked black claws. Dalton's mouth twisted into a gruesome smile that exposed long, sharp canines. He snarled her name and pounced. Julia screamed again as she heard him repeating her name in a deep, guttural growl. His claws ripped at her shoulder and white-hot pain seared through her. "No, Dalton," she screamed and tried to escape his hold on her.

"Jules," Dalton said, shaking her shoulder. Julia's green eyes, wet with tears, fluttered open, and she blinked at the light streaming through the window. "Wake up, Jules. You're having a nightmare."

Julia threw her arms around Dalton's neck, sobbing with relief. "Oh, Dalton, it's you."

"Who did you think it would be?" he gently brushed her hair out of her eyes and used his thumb to dab a tear from her pale cheek. "That must have been one hell of a nightmare," he said, chuckling softly as he wrapped her in his muscular arms. "I'm here, and it's OK."

Comfortable in his arms, Julia collected herself. She pulled back, sniffing her nose. "What time is it? How long have I been asleep? I don't even remember coming home and going to bed." Julia gazed around the room to make sure she was in her house and not still trapped in the horrible dream.

"It's a quarter past five. You were asleep when I got home an hour ago. I was going to let you sleep until six. Tell me about that dream. I was in the kitchen getting things ready to go to your mom's when I heard you scream bloody murder."

Julia jerked out of his arms. "Damn. The potluck. I didn't

mean to sleep this long," she said as she tried to scramble off the bed.

"It's all set to go, Jules. I packed up the eggs in a tray, put that fruit salad you cut up into a container, and put beers from the case I bought on ice." Dalton ran a reassuring hand over her curly red head. "You just get your face back on and your hair fixed. I'll put everything into the car."

She glanced at her reflection in the mirror above her dresser and cringed. Black mascara streaked her face. "Oh, my goodness. I look a-fright." Julia slid from the bed to her feet and shuffled to the bathroom. Incense smoked on her altar, the same incense from her dream. In the bathroom, she used a wet-wipe to cleanse the mascara from her face. She didn't replace it, but she did reapply her lipstick.

Walking into the kitchen and seeing Dalton standing at the counter brought back her terrible dream. It took all of Julia's strong will to take the first step into the room where an ice chest and an open case of Bud Longnecks sat on the table.

"I thought you said it was all in the car," she said tentatively. Julia watched as Dalton turned to her and stood ready to flee, but the face greeting her with a sweet smile was that of *her* Dalton and not the hideous *loup-garou*. She couldn't fathom where her mind had conjured that face, possibly an amalgam of Hollywood portrayals. She couldn't help but give a mental sigh of relief, however.

"I thought you might like a beer before we left." Dalton opened the cooler, took out two brown glass bottles with their red, white, and blue labels, and handed one to her.

"Thanks, babe. It's just what I need." She popped off the cap and took a long refreshing drink of the cold beer. "That's perfect," Julia sighed out, and smiled.

"Now tell me about that nightmare. I've never heard anyone scream in their sleep the way you did. It scared the shit out of me."

Julia shrugged her shoulders and took another quick sip.

"I'm not sure when my day ended, and the nightmare began. I was at work, and my drawer was over, so I had to stay and do a recount. Then I drove home. I'm pretty sure all of that happened, but this is where it gets weird." She took another drink, worried about how Dalton would take the next part. "I walked into the house, and I smelled the incense. You were in the kitchen at the counter. I was telling you how nice it was of you to light the incense and when you turned around, it wasn't you."

"What do you mean, it wasn't me? Who was it that scared you so bad?"

"It was a *loup-garou*," Julia said nervously. "He started coming after me, and that's when I screamed. He was calling my name and tearing at my shoulder. I thought he was going to rip my arm off."

Dalton sat quietly for a few minutes, and it worried Julia. After his statement the morning before that he thought she didn't want to make love to him because of the curse, Julia couldn't help but worry.

"Well, I lit the incense while you were sleeping," he finally said. "You probably smelled it, and I was messing around in the kitchen. You probably heard it, and your brain twisted it into something else. After I heard you scream, I came running and tried to shake you awake by your shoulder. I must have grabbed it too hard. I'm so sorry if I hurt you."

"No, babe." Julia took his hand. He made the dream sound logical, and it eased her mind. "You've got nothing to be sorry about. It was just a stupid nightmare. I didn't sleep much last night and then had a discrepancy in my drawer at work. It was just a stress dream."

"Yeah, but I'm the one stressing you. If it weren't for me, all of this wouldn't have fallen on your shoulders."

"Oh, bullshit," she said, trying to sound reassuring. "It's fucking Althea Rubidoux and her coven. They've been breaking High Council laws for years, but my grandmother and mother let them get by with it because nobody out here wants the High Council in their business."

"Yeah, I don't get that. If y'all aren't breakin' any Council Laws and the Rubidoux Coven is, why not let this De la Croix come in and clean it all up?"

"Well, if truth be told," Julia said, "some of the DuBois have been known to *bend* Council Laws from time to time, and they'd just as soon not have it brought to light with an investigation into the Rubidoux. It all goes back hundreds of years. We can talk about it another time." Julia picked up the partial case of beer. "We need to get going now."

They drove in silence to the DuBois mansion, where Julia parked in front of the garage as the drive once again held a multitude of vehicles. They didn't see Bernard's Lexus.

"I guess big brother isn't back from New Orleans yet," Dalton sneered.

"I've been thinking about it, babe, and I don't think we should give up that piece of knowledge quite yet. I know you're pissed, but let's just keep it to ourselves for the time being. My parents aren't in good health, and they don't need that kind of upset on top of everything else." Julia patted his hand and hoped he understood.

Dalton stretched across the center console and kissed Julia soundly on the mouth. "I understand, Jules, but I'm still gonna kick his sorry ass the first chance I get." Dalton straightened in his seat and released the seatbelt. "I think that bitch must have been fucking your brother while she was fucking me, and then she goes and puts a damned curse on *me* for finding somebody else."

"You're probably right. Now that I think back on it, Bernard has been away on business a lot in the past few months." Julia got the beer and the plastic tub of fruit salad from the back seat, leaving the tray of eggs in the cooler for Dalton to carry. "Careful of the cooler. We don't want our deviled eggs scrambled."

"No worries," Dalton assured her, "I know how to pack a cooler."

At the back gate, they were greeted by Julia's parents, who'd heard the car. Ruby DuBois touched Dalton's shoulder as he passed through the gate. "It's all right to shake the boy's hand tonight, Ben. The Residual is manageable now."

Dalton followed them past the group on the patio and into the spacious kitchen. "There are deviled eggs on ice in the cooler. Do you want me to get them out?"

"Oh, gracious, no," Ruby told him. "Go on out with the others. Julia and I can put this all together. We'll call y'all when it's ready."

"Come on, son," Ben DuBois said, slapping Dalton on the back in a fatherly manner. "When those two women say get out of their kitchen, you'd best run." The frail man extended his hand to Dalton. "I'm Ben DuBois. Sorry, I couldn't shake your hand last week, but Ruby was right. My old heart isn't what it once was, and the strong Residual would have been dangerous."

Dalton took Ben's hand. "Dalton La Pierre, sir. It's nice to meet you officially." Dalton gave a nervous pause, wondering what he should say next to the father of the woman he was sleeping with out of wedlock.

Ben DuBois smiled as he took Dalton's hand. "There's no need to search for words on that account, boy," Julia's father said with a chuckle. "We don't exactly follow the same moral codes as our Judeo-Christian counterparts here in the South. We believe two consenting adults can do as they see fit with their bodies. Our philosophy is to do what you will so long as it harms no other." The old man walked with Dalton to find a chair.

"That's one reason my daughter had to go to the High Council in New Orleans about the Rubidoux Coven. Not only have they broken High Council Law by casting the *loup-garou* upon you, but they've also gone against one of our deepest principles and done you harm with their magic. It's unforgivable to those of us who still adhere to the Reade."

"Thank you, sir, but I think I'm in love with your daughter and will do everything I can to protect and care for her."

People to either side of them who'd heard Dalton's declaration broke out into laughter. Dalton looked at Ben DuBois in confusion. The old man began laughing as well. "Boy, my daughter is the High Priestess of the DuBois. She can channel more power from her little finger than is in a nuclear warhead. A High Priestess of DuBois needs no protection from any man." He slapped Dalton's knee. "But I'm sure she's going to appreciate you saying it."

The evening progressed through the dinner of regular potluck fare like potato salad, mac and cheese, slaw, as well as Julia's deviled eggs and fruit salad. Desserts of Jell-O, peach cobbler and German Chocolate cake graced the big island in the DuBois kitchen. Ben grilled tender ribeye to everyone's liking, and when the meal had been cleaned up, Dalton felt like a tick ready to burst. Bernard and Terry DuBois arrived in time for dessert.

As the meeting finally gave way to the subject at hand, Julia took over. She transformed into a picture of authority and control. For the first time, Dalton got an inkling of why Ben and the others laughed at him for resolving to protect her.

Julia told them all what she'd read about the counter-curse of the *loup-garou* and the long list of ingredients needed. "I've put the matter of collecting those ingredients into Mary and Hal's capable hands, and I'm going to turn it over to them now." Julia took a seat beside Dalton, and the rotund couple rose to stand before the fire.

Mary, dressed in a moo-moo made of dark green fabric, looked to Dalton like a walking military issue tent.

"I've been over this list, and most of it can be found easy enough around here. The wolf's bane and silver solution to keep you," she looked awkwardly toward Dalton, "from going into the change I have at home and will prepare. I've already spoken with a few of you, and you know what to look for and where. Terry has been kind enough to volunteer Bernard and herself to collect honeysuckle nectar," she said with a smile and a wink at Bernard's wife. "We're going to need a good bit of it, so you two may be out in the sticks for the better part of the day. Pack a lunch and take a blanket to spread on the ground." Everyone laughed at what she implied.

Julia leaned over to whisper into Dalton's ear. "When they were first dating, Bernard and Terry would go off into the bayou with any silly excuse, but everyone knew they were screwing. They did it once without a blanket, and Bernard got poison ivy on his cock and balls," she giggled.

"Oh, my," Dalton said, and found it necessary to readjust his position in the chair.

"Yeah, it swelled up so bad my mom was worried it might have left him infertile," she snickered. "But I have a healthy niece and a nephew, so I guess it didn't do any damage after all."

The laughter at Bernard's expense settled down, and Mary continued. "I only have one problem area. The spell calls for a particular mushroom. It's rare, but it does grow around here. I won't give you the Latin name, but we always called them Pixie Arrows when I was a kid. Is anyone familiar with them? They grow to be about three inches tall on a fragile stem. The cap is a cone shape with a sharp point. They're very dark brown; almost black." Mary waited for someone to volunteer knowledge of the rare fungus.

Dalton stood. "I know what they are. My grandpa and I used to hunt up on the north bend of the Vermillion, and they grew thick there. My grandpa used to collect them to dry and grind up for rat poison in the barn."

"Your grandpa knew what he was about, then. They're deadly to critters like mice and rats when you dry them, grind them into a powder, and sprinkle the powder over food the pest likes to eat. In larger doses, they are deadly to humans, as well. Did you say you know where they grow?"

"Yeah, I used to deer hunt with him up there. I think I could find it again."

"That's perfect then. You and Julia make up my final team of foragers. I'll give her the estimated amount we'll need, and if you can find a few extra, that would be great," the big woman said. "It's always better to have too many than not enough."

With that, the meeting broke up, and people began filtering out. Dalton said hello to Terry DuBois but would not meet Bernard's gaze. As if sensing a problem, Dalton saw Bernard with Julia backed into a corner speaking in harsh tones. Dalton wandered their way and caught a snippet of the conversation.

"I don't know why you brought this man into our world in the first place, Julia," Bernard chided his younger sister. "You talk about Althea breaking Council Law, but you think it's all right to go and blab all our secrets to this outsider."

"Shut up, Bernard." Julia shook her brother's hand from her arm. "It's always been that way when one of us takes an outsider as our mate. You brought Terry into the family, just like half the people here have, so stop giving me shit about it."

"Just because you're the High and Mighty now, little sister, don't go getting a big head. Mom and Dad always gave you everything as the next High Priestess of the DuBois. This house will go to you when they're gone, but you don't appreciate it and choose to live in a sharecropper's shack in the Bottoms rather than with your own. Now you've given yourself to an uneducated grease-monkey. I don't understand you, Julia. I just don't understand."

"Is that what's chapped your ass, Bernard, that I'll inherit this monstrosity?" Julia's hand flew up to indicate the mansion. "You can have it, but I hope you know what you're getting into. This house is almost two hundred years old. The plumbing is shot, the electrical system is fried, and it needs a new roof. This place has nearly put Dad into his grave. He's spent almost everything he's ever made on the upkeep of this house and grounds. He's always made just enough to do it. Can you say that Bernard? You manage a Dollar General Store. What does that pay? It can't be much more than a whopping thirty-five grand. Dad made three times that, and Mom had the family trust. There's nothing left in the trust, Bernard."

"What are you talking about, Julia? The DuBois Trust was supposed to be worth millions. It can't possibly be gone. You're lying because you want it for yourself like the greedy, spoiled bitch you've always been."

"The Trust was worth millions before the crash in '08. That took almost all of it, and that finance manager granddaddy hired before he died filched the rest. If you want this falling down pile of bricks moldering in the swamp, you're welcome to it, Bernard. I'll tell Mom and Dad, but I think they already know that I have no interest in it."

Dalton watched Bernard storm off, grab Terry by the arm and pull her toward the door.

## 9

Two days after the meeting and her dust-up with Bernard, Julia, and Dalton prepared for a day out in the fresh air. Julia packed them lunch, and Dalton filled the cooler with bottles of water and beer. They drove in his truck to a dock on the Vermillion River, where Dalton rented one of the big airboats for the day. He told Julia they could probably make it up the river in a regular boat, but the summer had been dry, and some spots might be shallow. He assured her the airboat would be more fun as they loaded their gear on board.

"It's about an hour's ride upriver. Then we're going to have to hike for a good hour if I remember correctly. It's pretty damned remote. I haven't been up there in ten or twelve years, and storm damage may have changed the markers along the river as I remember them."

Julia swatted a mosquito. "Well, let's be on our way. That part of the Bayou is well into Rubidoux territory, and I'd like to get in and out as quickly as possible." She belted herself in, and Dalton started the engine, running the big fan that would push them along over the water.

They traveled along the waterway for close to an hour at a high rate of speed before Dalton finally powered down and slowed the boat. As they floated in the green water, he saw Julia gazing at alligators sunning themselves on the muddy banks. They saw distinct slides into the water used by the beasts. He smiled as Julia snugged her belt and gripped her seat. Dalton had to agree that it would be a terrible place to go into the water.

"Do you recognize anything?" Julia asked as Dalton scanned the river ahead intently.

"Yeah, I think so. See that big dead tree up ahead?" Dalton pointed to a massive dead tree towering above all the rest.

"It's an old cypress," Julia said. "I'm surprised nobody has harvested it. It's beautiful and expensive wood."

"My grandpa called it Old Man Tree. He told me that tree was probably a sprout when Moses parted the Red Sea."

Julia laughed. "He very well could have been right. Some of those big cypresses are known to be hundreds of years old. Who's to say it's not thousands? I know I don't want to be the one tasked with counting the rings."

"I hear that," Dalton agreed and shifted the boat to make their way to Old Man Tree. "Look," he pointed to the exposed root ball of the old tree. "One more big blow and Old Man Tree is gonna be swimmin'."

"That's a shame. How much farther from here?"

"Once we pass Old Man Tree, it gets shallow. Keep an eye out for a big pile of sandstone boulders. Just past the rocks is where grandpa used to anchor our boat."

Fifteen minutes later, Julia yanked on his sleeve and pointed to the pile of orangey-red boulders. Julia told him she had never seen rocks that large exposed in the bayou. They passed the majestic stones, and Dalton slowed the boat as he looked for a place to anchor or run up onto the shore. He found a spot free of rocks or dead tree limbs and slid the airboat upon dry land far enough that they could step off without getting their feet wet.

"This is about where we used to leave our boat. We'd pitch a tent in the first really dry spot we found."

"This all looks pretty dry to me," Julia said, looking around at brown grasses and withered ferns.

"It's been a dry summer. Keep an eye out for snakes, but as dry as it is, they're probably sticking close to the river."

"I will, but I packed a snake bite kit just in case. Which way do we go to find the mushrooms? Do you think there will even be any if it's so dry?"

"If I remember right, they grow in a wooded spot at a bend in a creek that feeds into the river. It's damp there even in summers with little rain. They grow in the old fallen leaves. The first time I ever saw them, they were really thick and looked like a tiny black forest. I thought it was so cool. My grandpa said it was where the Pixies lived and not ever to get cross-wise of a Pixie because they were mean little shits." Dalton suddenly stopped and looked at her.

"What? Why did we stop?" Julia asked.

"Don't tell me that Pixies and Faeries really do exist." Dalton stared at her with an awed expression.

Julia held her sides laughing. "Dalton, some stories are just stories. As far as I know, there are no Pixies or Faeries, not in Louisiana, anyhow." She began to walk again. "And there's no Santa Clause or Easter Bunny either."

"Well, that sucks. Why are there no *good* supernatural creatures? Why are there only the bad ones?"

"Do you think I'm bad?" Julia pushed her lower lip out in an exaggerated pout.

"Nah. It's like in *The Wizard of Oz*. You're Glinda the Good Witch, and Althea is The Wicked Witch of the West." Dalton's smile suddenly faded. "Please tell me she doesn't have fucking flying monkeys."

"She does not have flying monkeys or ruby slippers either," Julia assured him. "What she does have are coven members who are scared shitless of her and will do almost anything she tells them to do."

"That may be even worse than flying monkeys." Dalton took a bottle of water from his pack.

They walked for almost an hour, and the tall grasses had turned into thorny scrub and spiny saw palmettos. Julia had dozens of snags and cuts on her hands and several rips on her jeans.

"Damn, Dalton, why didn't you tell me we'd be hiking through razor blades?" Julia sucked at a cut on her thumb that wouldn't stop bleeding.

Dalton suddenly felt uneasy. He could smell the coppery blood, but he could smell something else as well. He took a few steps away from Julia, hoping that putting distance between himself and her blood would calm him. From the shadows of nearby trees, Dalton saw men moving in their direction. They wore torn and dirty clothes, and they looked as though they hadn't seen barbers in months or years even. Their matted and dirty hair hung down around their faces, and shaggy beards covered their faces.

Dalton lunged for Julia and pulled her to him, ignoring the annoying scent of her blood. Peering at the approaching men, Dalton felt an inexplicable need to make them aware that Julia was his. The breeze carried the feral scent of the men, and Dalton bared his teeth.

"What is it?" Julia asked as Dalton pulled her tightly into his sweaty chest.

"Look," he said and pointed toward the approaching group. "They don't look friendly. Are they Rubidoux?"

"I don't think so. Dalton, you're hurting me." Julia tried to break from his grasp. "Let me go."

"No. You're mine, and I'm not going to let them have you." Dalton gripped Julia's arm tighter.

"What are you talking about, Dalton?" Julia pulled free of him. "I don't belong to you or anybody else. Get a grip and calm down. Let's just see who they are and what they want."

"They want you," Dalton snarled and stepped between her and the approaching men.

He and Julia stood quietly until the men stopped about ten yards from them. Dalton could smell them. Their scent filled his nose and overwhelmed his senses. He could smell their lust for Julia and knew they could smell him.

One man stepped forward, smiling through his thick black facial hair. "Hello. Are you here to join the pack?" He stared at Julia and licked his lips. "It's good of you to bring a female. We haven't had a female in some time. We could all use a good fuck."

"The female is mine," Dalton snarled, baring his teeth.

"Sure, friend, but we share and share alike out here. If she's the only female in the pack, then she gets fucked by all of us unless you want to fight for her." Dalton watched the others moving slowly forward and widening the distances between them to encircle him and Julia.

Julia stepped around Dalton. "What the hell are you talking about?" she demanded, and Dalton sensed a power radiating from Julia he'd never felt before. "What is this pack business, and what are all y'all doing out here in the bayou? Where do you live?" She raised a hand toward the advancing men. "Somebody tell me what is going on out here. Now!" With that, the man who'd come forward cringed and fell back with the others who'd grouped together again. "Someone speak," Julia demanded.

"You're a witch," someone said. "Be on your way. We don't want any more trouble with witches.

"Come here," Julia commanded, and a man in torn slacks and the remnants of a blazer stepped forward. "Who are you people, and what are you doing here?"

"I'm Norman Potete, and these are my brothers in misery. Were you sent here by Althea to check up on us?"

"Norm Potete?" Julia stepped forward and studied the man. "Your family has been looking for you for more than a year.

What are you doing out here, and what does Althea Rubidoux have to do with it?"

"This motley crew is my family now," he said, gesturing toward the men behind him. "Althea Rubidoux is the hateful bitch who forced us to live here like this."

"But how and why?" Julia asked.

Norm stepped past Julia to stand before Dalton. "He knows. He's one of us now. She and her bunch have cursed him, too."

Julia took a sharp breath and stared at the men gathered together in a tight group. "You mean you're all *loup-garou?* How? She gasped in horror at the plight of the men. "Why?"

"Most of them are here because they were dating her and dumped her bitch ass," he said. "A couple of the other guys and I pissed her off over business deals. There were two women amongst us for a while, but they died. Luther, over there, is her own cousin. He's never really said why he's here, but he was the first of us."

"Norm Potete of Potete Porsche?" Dalton asked with wide eyes. "Everyone thinks you ran off because of a woman."

"I did," he huffed, "Althea Rubidoux. I turned down her credit application for a car, and the next thing I know,, I'm waking up covered in blood with her standing over me laughing her head off. She tells me I can come out here or go home and chance killing my wife and kids when the moon is full again."

A shaggy-haired blonde man stepped forward. "I'm Larry Peters, and I refused to give her a loan from the bank where I worked. The same as with Norm." He stared with pleading eyes at Julia and Dalton. "Do you know my wife, Annie Peters? She has breast cancer and was in treatment when I came out here nine moons ago."

Julia had known Annie Peters. "I'm sorry, Mr. Peters, your wife died two months ago." Julia told Dalton later that she hadn't known Larry Peters, but she remembered when he'd disappeared. She'd only been working at the bank for a couple of months when the man had simply stopped showing up at work.

Everyone thought he'd crumbled under the pressure of his job as a senior loan officer there and his wife's failing health.

Dalton heard his mournful howl and watched Larry Peters fall to the ground. Some of the others tried to help him back to his feet, but he waved them off as tears streamed from his eyes to disappear into his thick growth of facial hair.

Julia stepped forward again. "Gentlemen, I'm Julia DuBois, and I'm here to gather some mushrooms to use in a counter-curse to restore Dalton here back to normal." There was excited murmuring amongst the men.

"She's lying," someone thundered, "there is no counter-spell for this. It's permanent. Once you've been turned, the only countermeasure for this condition is death."

"How do you know that?" Julia asked the faceless voice in the crowd.

"I know because I'm Luther Rubidoux and that bitch Althea is my cousin. My mother was the last Mother of the Coven, and Althea killed her in order to take her place."

Dalton couldn't say why, but he could smell deceit oozing from the man. He bent to whisper into Julia's ear. "He's lying, Jules. I can't explain how I know, but I can *smell* it. He's lying."

Julia stepped into the circle of men to face Luther, a small man with African American features and scarred, light brown skin. His round brown eyes widened when Julia put both hands upon his shoulders. "Speak the truth Luther Rubidoux. How did you come to reside here with the cursed?"

Luther's eyes rolled back into his head, and he began to tremble and twitch.

"Stop fighting the compulsion and speak the truth," Julia commanded.

His twitching stopped, and he slumped. "Althea promised me a place at her side if I helped her kill my mother," Luther admitted. "I gave her a box of chocolates Althea had prepared and given to me. They were poisoned with the Pixie Arrow mushrooms. I watched my mother die an agonizing death and then called Althea to claim my prize. When I went to her with my mother's ritual chest, holding the Rubidoux Grimoire, Althea accused me before the entire coven of killing my mother and sentenced me to this exile. They turned me and brought me here. She made me promise to spy on these mangy curs and report back to her if any of them tried to leave the glen. Althea promised me a place of power at her side, but she lied."

He broke down weeping, and several of the men began to kick him.

"Stop," Julia commanded. "He's scum, but he's still in the same boat as all of you. How many of you have been here for less than a year?"

Dalton watched seven men, including Larry Peters, raise their hands. The wailing Luther Rubidoux did not raise his.

"I'm sorry, but those of you who've made twelve turns cannot be changed back. I don't know whether my Coven can save the rest of you, but we will try. Dalton and I have come here to collect Pixie Arrows to use in the spell to reverse his curse. If any of you know where they grow, could you help us to find them?" Julia took out her phone, pulled up the calculator feature, and figured how much she would need for seven additional victims. "According to my botanist's calculations, we'll need about forty of the mushrooms to have enough. If you can find more, it would be great."

"I know where they grow," said one of the six who could not be saved. "Do you have a bucket or a bag to put them in?"

Dalton pulled a folded brown paper lunch sack from his back pocket. Julia gave him a questioning look.

"My grandpa said to only put them into brown paper sacks you could burn. They'll poison anything else, and it will be poisoned forever.

"That's true," Luther confirmed, "and don't touch them with your hands. Their poison will seep, right through the skin.

Dalton dug into his pack and pulled out a box of latex gloves.

He handed them to Julia and shrugged. "Grandpa always brought rubber gloves."

Julia passed the gloves and the paper sack to the man who'd said he knew where to find the mushrooms. "Thank you, and what is your name?"

"I'm Stephen Matisse, and I won't need the gloves. I'd rather die of the poison than continue the way I have for the past sixteen moons. Would you tell my mother that you found me and that I died with honor? Tell her I said she was right about Althea Rubidoux and that I'm sorry I ever doubted her. My mother is Mrs. Myra Matisse of Covington."

"I know who she is, Stephen. She's spent thousands searching for you."

"Thank you, Miss DuBois. I wish you luck saving my brothers here. We've hunted together, cried together, and promised to stand together. Aside from that miserable fool Luther, they're all honorable men who elected to live out here rather than take the chance of harming others." He took the bag. "I'll be back." He turned toward the shadowy woods.

One of the others took him by the shoulder. "Wait up, Steve, we're coming with you." Five other men, including Luther Rubidoux, joined him. Dalton, holding Julia's trembling hand, watched the group of men disappear into the shadows.

Infuriated, Julia dug in her pack for her phone. When her fingers finally found it, she latched onto it and yanked it out. She checked it for a signal and saw one bar. She pounded in the key to connect with Antoine De la Croix.

"De la Croix here. How may I help you?"

"This is Julia DuBois, Mr. De la Croix, and I have some further information regarding Althea Rubidoux and her coven."

"Miss DuBois, I've been in contact with an associate in your region, and I'm told you and Miss Rubidoux have been contending for the affections of the same man, and this is no more than a matter of two women fussing over the same pretty piece of fluff. I'm not interested in wasting my time with such nonsense," Antione De la Croix chided in his deep, booming voice.

"She's cast the *loup-garou* on thirteen other men and two women in the past two years, and she murdered Eleanor Rubidoux to assume her position in the coven. Wasn't Eleanor your cousin?"

"Miss DuBois, if I find that you're using my affection for my late cousin to prod me into a bogus investigation, I will have you *and* your coven sanctioned. What makes you think somebody murdered my cousin?"

"Her son Luther is one of the thirteen men I just discovered hidden out in the bayou, and he admitted that he helped Althea poison his mother using chocolates laced with Pixie Arrows. Althea promised him a position at her side leading the Rubidoux Coven, but instead, she accused him of the poisoning and the coven cast the curse upon him as a punishment. I'd imagine she's used that casting as a sword over the head of her coven to coerce them into these other castings."

"Luther is there? Let me speak to the little bastard," De la Croix demanded. "I want to hear it from his mouth."

"He and a few of the men went on a suicide mission of sorts."

"I beg your pardon?" De la Croix asked gruffly in his deep baritone.

"I need Pixie Arrows for the counter curse and Luther along with the other men here who have made more than twelve changes elected to collect the mushrooms." Julia waited, but De la Croix did not speak. "They're collecting them without protection for their hands."

"I see," he sighed out. "They're making the noble sacrifice. Do you expect them to return soon?"

"I have no idea, Mr. De la Croix."

"Well, if they return alive, call me back." De la Croix disconnected.

"What a prick," Julia muttered.

Julia punched in Mary's number to tell her they'd need seven times more ingredients for the counter-curse but got no answer. "Mary and Hal must be out of cell service," she told Dalton. "I'll try to get Peggy and Tom."

"I'd be surprised if you can get any of them. I can't believe you've got bars out here."

"We're only a few miles downriver from Covington, I think. I'm probably catching a cell tower from up there." Julia listened to Peggy's phone ring and was about to hang up when someone finally answered.

"Is that you, Julia?" Tom, Peggy's husband, asked in a frantic voice.

"Yeah, Tom, it's me. What's going on?"

"You need to get back here right quick. There's been an attack on our foraging parties." There was a long pause. "It's bad, Julia, real bad."

"What kind of attack, Tom? What do you mean?" Julia asked loud enough to turn Dalton's head away from his conversation.

"Mary and Hal were beaten up badly. Mick and Franny were also hurt, but we got them back to your mom's, and she's patched them up, but we can't get hold of the other groups." He ended with a pause.

"What else, Tom?"

"I got a 911 from your brother," Tom said slowly, "but I couldn't get him or Terry back. They were supposed to be going up the east side of Black Bayou, but I don't know exactly how far. Mary said there was an old plum thicket up there some-where covered up with honeysuckle. She sent them out there to collect the honeysuckle nectar we need."

Julia ran a trembling hand through her red curls. "I know where it is, but I'm miles from there. I'm an hour's hike from our boat and then another hour up the Vermillion from our truck." Julia gave Dalton a worried look. He shrugged his shoulders back at her questioning. "Once we get back to the truck, I can get over there from the docks in about forty-five minutes, but that's going to be a good three hours from now. Can you get someone else? The thicket is just off Parish Road one ten east, about three or four miles off the main road out of St. Elizabeth. It's on the old Métiers place back behind that big old barn."

"Oh, yeah. I remember where that is. We picked wild plums there when I was a kid. I'll get out there right away. I'll call you when I know something." Tom paused again. "What were *you* calling for? Are you and Dalton all right? Did you find your mushrooms?"

"Yes, and we found more than that." Julia coughed to clear her throat and suppress her worry about the others. "We found thirteen other men Althea and her coven have cursed with the *loup-garou*. They've been living out here in the bayou away from civilization." Julia took a breath. "One of them is Luther Rubidoux, Eleanor's son."

"Are you shittin' me?" Tom gasped. "What the hell's been goin' on with that damned coven?"

"It's a long story, Tom, but only seven of these guys can be saved. We're going to need a whole lot more of the ingredients for the counter curse to help them all."

"I'll let your mom know on my way out to find your brother and Terry. Just get back here as soon as you can, Julia. We need you."

"I'm on my way as soon as I get those mushrooms, Tom. Let Mom and Dad know I'm okay."

"I will," Tom said and closed their connection.

"What is it, Jules?" Dalton asked as soon as she took her phone from her ear. "What's happened?"

"Our people have been attacked. Mary and Hal were hurt but got back to Mom and Dad's. Bernard sent a 911 call, and nobody's been able to get them on the phone again. The other teams are out of communication, as well. Tom is on his way to look for Bernard and Terry now. Oh, Dalton." Julia fell into his arms, sobbing softly. His warm embrace soothed her, and she began to collect her jumbled thoughts as someone announced the return of the men who'd gone foraging for the Pixie Arrows.

Julia looked up to see the group of shaggy men moving at a run through the high grasses of the clearing.

"They're afraid," Dalton whispered. "I can *smell* it on them. Look at the others, Jules. They can smell it too."

Julia looked over to the group of men who'd stayed behind.

They huddled together but searched warily about with their eyes. All the men had their shaggy heads lifted, sniffing the air.

Norm, leading the group of foragers, came running up panting. He handed Julia the paper sack, heavy with mushrooms. She couldn't help noticing his blackened fingertips and palms as he released his grip on the bag. "There are people in boats along the creek. They're looking for you two."

Luther Rubidoux stepped forward. "They're Rubidoux Coven members sent to keep you from collecting the Pixie Arrows. Althea knows you need them, and she knows this is the only place to find them. Y'all better get movin' before they find your boat."

All the men looked pale and sweat beaded on their foreheads. Julia suspected the poison had begun to take effect. Luther, the smallest of them, started coughing, and Julia saw blood on his lips. The poison was progressing faster in him.

Julia punched in the number for Antoine De la Croix and hoped he'd answer.

"Hello, Miss DuBois," De la Croix answered in an exasperated tone. "Has Luther returned?"

"Yes, but you'd better get his testimony quickly. He doesn't have much time left. The Pixie Arrows are working on him fast." She handed the phone to Luther. "Your cousin Antoine wants to talk to you." Julia stood close to listen to Luther's side of the conversation.

"Hello," Luther said, trembling from fear of the man on the phone, she suspected, as much as from the effects of the poison. "No, she's telling you the truth. I helped Althea kill Mama." Julia watched the small man clench his eyes shut. "I know, and I'm sorry. I'm so, so sorry, sir. Yes, it was Althea's idea. She told me we'd share power over the coven." He paused, and his face looked pained, then irritated.

"What damned money?" Luther shouted. "There ain't any Rubidoux money left. I guess she thought there was still money, but Mama spent that up years ago. The family's in debt up to its ears tryin' to keep up that ridiculous chateau out there on the island."

Luther coughed again, spraying blood all over her phone. He fell to his knees. "I can't. This phone is poison now that I've touched it. You should know that Althea's sent out people to stop her from getting the things they need to counter the curse. I could hear them talking from where we were hiding. They said it was a shoot-on-sight order. I know. It's the only good thing about this damned curse. We all have better hearing and smell. Yeah, OK, goodbye, Mr. De la Croix, sir. I'll tell her." Luther clicked off the phone but didn't hand it back to Julia.

"Cousin Antoine said to tell you he would deal with Althea and the Rubidoux Coven appropriately." He looked down at the blood-spattered phone still clutched in his trembling hand. "Would you mind if the others used this to call their families to say goodbye?"

"Not at all. It's getting some signal, and it's fully charged. Be my guest." Julia turned her back on the coughing men with tears of pity and rage in her eyes. Had she or Althea just killed these men?

Dalton picked up the paper sack of mushrooms. "We'll be back for you guys when it's time for the ritual." Dalton shrugged off his pack. "There are bottles of water, some beers, and a little food in here. Come on, babe," he said, putting his free arm around Julia's slumped shoulders, "let's get you home to your people."

## 11

---

D alton helped Julia maneuver through the thick brambles
and tall grass on the hour-long hike back toward the boat.
He hoped Althea's thugs hadn't found it and wrecked it. If they
had, the bastards would probably be waiting to ambush them as
they returned. With any luck, they were in a regular boat and
wouldn't be able to maneuver the shallows where he and Julia
had landed. Dalton doubted a motorboat would make it past the
sandstone outcropping, and if they couldn't, they wouldn't be
able to see the airboat pushed up on the bank where he'd left it.

"Slow down, Jules," he told her in a hushed tone, "I want to
make certain Althea's people haven't found the boat. That's why
we've been hugging this tree line instead of walking across the
field. I wanted to keep us out of their line of sight if they've
found it." Dalton had also wanted to keep close to the shade
rather than marching for an hour under the direct sun, where
they'd be moving targets.

"That was a good idea," Julia told him. "Can you see the boat
yet?" She craned her neck to look in the direction she thought
the river should be. "We should be getting close to the river."

Dalton pointed a bit to the right of where Julia stared intently.
"There's the pile of boulders. I can just see the boat's bow, but I

can't see much more than that. We'll start cutting across here to the rocks. If they're going to ambush us, they'd be using the rocks for cover. We'll be coming up behind them this way." He put a finger to his lips to indicate he wanted her to remain quiet as they moved through the tall grass.

Dalton broke branches from a dead tree and handed one to Julia. "For snakes," he whispered. "We're close to the river now." Julia nodded in understanding. They walked slowly, brushing the concealing grass around them with the long sticks. When they came to the bank of the river, Dalton peeked through the dense growth to look for another boat upon the water or people walking along the muddy edge of the river. He saw neither and breathed a heavy sigh. To his relief, he didn't see any concealed gators either.

"Come on," he said softly, "let's make for the rocks and the boat. I think we're clear, but let's keep it quiet just to be safe."

Julia began to walk toward the sandstone outcrop. Dalton stopped dead in his tracks when he heard the distant whine of an outboard motor.

"What?" Julia asked when he stopped ahead of her. "I don't hear anything," she whispered, shaking her head and pointing to her ear.

"Must be the enhanced wolf thing Luther was talking about. I can hear a motor and men's voices back down the river." Dalton jerked his head to indicate the river in the direction that they'd have to travel to get back to the dock and truck. "It sounds like it's moving away. Maybe they're traveling back up that creek those guys were talking about."

"I hope so," Julia said, then took off at a steady pace toward their boat.

Dalton helped Julia into her seat, then stowed their remaining pack and the bag of dearly bought mushrooms. He pushed the boat back into the water and started the engine. Maneuvering it around in the shallows to get them headed back down the river took a bit of doing, but Dalton managed it and soon had the boat flying over the water.

He breathed a sigh of relief when they passed the mouth of the narrow creek and saw no bushwhackers waiting for them. Once they'd passed Old Man Tree, Dalton gave the boat full throttle. They had to slow for a few fishermen but didn't get stopped by anyone with shotguns or rifles. Dalton remembered hearing Luther tell the person on the phone that Althea had ordered her people to shoot-on-sight.

"Do you think we're safe now?" Julia asked when they'd slowed to pass a boat of men hunting the edge of the river for alligators.

"I think so." He smiled. "We should be back at the dock in about fifteen minutes. How are you doing?" Dalton reached over and brushed Julia's arm affectionately.

"I'm beat, and I'm worried about Bernard and Terry, but I'm OK."

When they reached the dock, Dalton floated to the fuel pump to gas up the boat, helped Julia out, and handed her the pack and small cooler to carry to the truck. "Here's the key. Go ahead and get in. I'll finish up in the office and be right over."

"Can I borrow your phone to check in?" she asked him before he walked off.

"Sure." He handed Julia his phone and went into the office to pay for the fuel. "We're back, Lenny. I owe you twenty-three-fifty for fuel." Dalton took out his wallet and handed the older man behind the counter his MasterCard.

"You find what you was lookin' for upriver?" the man asked after taking the card and swiping it in the cash register. Dalton paused before answering. He didn't recall telling the man they were looking for anything. Lenny handed Dalton back his card along with the receipt to sign. He scribbled his signature and scooted it back across the counter. "Yep, found it, and then some," Dalton said with a mischievous grin. Was it possible old Lenny was in Althea's pocket or a member of her coven?

Before getting into the truck, Dalton peeked at the underside and popped the hood. After giving the engine a thorough check, he dropped the hood and climbed in.

"What was that all about?" Julia asked as he buckled his seatbelt.

"Lenny seemed to know we went upriver looking for something. He wanted to know if we'd found it. I just thought I should check the truck for surprises," he said and smiled. "You get your calls made?"

"No answer at Mom's." Julia said with worry, "and I couldn't remember Tom and Peggy's number. That's the problem with cell phones. You have all the numbers stored in the damned things and don't put anything to memory. I can remember when I knew everybody's numbers. Now I barely remember my own."

"I hear that," he said with a chuckle. "So, where to now? You wanna go to your dad's or out to where your brother and Terry were supposed to be?"

"Let's stop by Dad's first. It's on the way. If they're not home, then I'll leave a note and we can head out to the old barn."

They drove to the DuBois mansion to find the drive filled with cars, and Dalton parked around back. As if sensing trouble, Julia leaped from the truck as soon as Dalton had shifted into park and ran toward the house. With his newly discovered enhanced hearing, Dalton heard Julia's mournful wail from the drive and rushed into the crowded house to find Julia in tears wrapped in Mary's heavy, bruised arms.

"What's happened?" Dalton asked a man standing in the kitchen. He recognized the white head of Tom, the other botany expert of the coven, and the person Julia had spoken with earlier. Dalton thought he looked like an old hippie with his white hair hanging long over his boney shoulders.

"It's bad, man. It's really bad." He squeezed Dalton's upper arm with the affection of a beloved family member. Dalton could smell the man's genuine sympathy and grief over the loss of someone.

"When Julia said you guys were so far out, me and Peg went out to look for Bernard and Terry. We saw their car out there and walked back past the barn callin' for 'em." He took a deep breath. Dalton lent the man his arm.

"Thanks, man," he said, shaking his head. "I don't think I'm ever going to get that sight out of my head. On a quilt spread out on the grass with a bottle of wine and two glasses set next to it were Terry and Bernard, naked. They'd been stung to death by honey bees. Some were still stuck on their bodies. It looked as though Bernard had laid his body over Terry trying to shield her, but they were both stung so bad. Their eyes were swelled shut, and there were still bees in their mouths and noses. It was fucking horrible."

Dalton put an arm around the man's shoulders as he broke down in tears.

"Me and Peg got their bodies into the bed of our truck and brought them here." He began to sob. "We shouldn't have brought them here, though. We shouldn't have brought them here." Tom took a deep breath and wiped his eyes with his thin, calloused hands. "When Ben saw them, he collapsed. His heart gave out, and he died on the spot. Ruby collapsed too, but she's not dead. We called an ambulance, and they took her to the hospital. They think she may have had a mild stroke," Tom fumed, and Dalton's senses picked up the man's mood change from one of grief and despair to one of white-hot anger. "It wasn't the sight of the bodies or Ben's collapse that caused Ruby to stroke out, it was the damned Residual. Someone used strong magic to cause those bees to attack Bernard and Terry, and the Residual killed poor Ben."

Peggy came and took Tom into her arms. "Dalton," she said tenderly, "go to Julia. She needs you now, sweetie."

"Yes, ma'am." Dalton made his way over to Julia, who was still being rocked in Mary's massive arms. Dalton could see the big woman sported a black eye and had several large, dark bruises on her arms. When she saw Dalton standing before them, she took her arms from around the sobbing young woman and allowed him to take her.

"Come on, Jules. Let me take you home."

"No, I need to go see my mom, Dalton," Julia sobbed, burying her red head into his chest. "I need my mom. Take me to the hospital, please." Dalton lifted Julia to her feet on unsteady legs and carried her along through the milling people and out to his truck. He helped her in and buckled the seatbelt over her shoulder and across her heaving chest.

"I'm so sorry, Baby," Dalton said, kissing her softly. "I feel like tis is all my fault. I should have never brought you and your family into my feud with Althea."

Tears streamed from Julia's eyes. "This feud between the DuBois and the Rubidoux has been festering for centuries, Dalton," she sobbed, "but I intend to see it ended for good now."

## 12

J ulia sat numb to the world around her in Dalton's truck as
they drove to the St. Elizabeth Hospital. He helped her out
and held her hand as they walked to the information desk
in the lobby.

"I'm here to see my mother, Ruby DuBois," Julia told the
blue-haired woman behind the counter.

"Just a moment while I find her." Julia watched the woman
tap the keys of her computer and study the screen. "Your mother
is in room two-twelve. Just take the elevator up to the second
floor and make a left."

"Thank you," Julia sniffed and wiped her red, swollen eyes.
She didn't want her mother to see her looking defeated.

In the elevator, she leaned into Dalton's muscular body. She
was so grateful for his strength, but she felt a stab of guilt at this.
*She* should be the strong one now. Julia DuBois, mother of her
coven, shouldn't be a Weeping Willow. Her mother, her coven,
and Dalton needed her to be strong, but leaning into Dalton
right now felt so good. She only wanted to lean on him more,
and have his strength wrapped around her.

The elevator doors opened, and the acrid scents of antiseptics and floor cleaners assaulted her nose. They exited to the left, and Dalton halted her at the nurse's station.

"We're here to see Mrs. Ruby DuBois," he told the nurse sitting behind the desk. "The lady downstairs said she was in room two-twelve."

"Just down the hall there." A young nurse in a colorful floral smock told them. "They brought her supper a few minutes ago, but I don't think she's in a mood to eat. The EMTs thought she might have had a stroke, but we did an MRI and the doctor said it was just the anxiety over the loss of her husband and son. He gave her a mild sedative. She should be fine after a few days of rest."

"Thank you, miss," Dalton said, and led Julia to the wide door with the brass numbers two-twelve screwed onto it.

Julia rushed in to find her mother propped up on pillows and her eyes rimmed red from crying. When she saw her daughter, Ruby DuBois raised both thin arms and spread them wide. "Come here, baby." Julia rushed into her mother's outstretched arms. "It's just me and you now, sweetheart. Daddy and Bernard are gone," Ruby sobbed with her face buried in Julia's red curls. "They took both of them and sweet little Terry, too."

"I know, Mommy. I know."

Dalton pushed a chair behind Julia so she could sit, but she remained standing bent over her sobbing mother while Dalton looked on from behind.

"Mary told me what happened. I'm so sorry for bringing all of this down on our heads," Julia said before her legs collapsed, and she found herself sitting. "Maybe I should have left well enough alone like you and Grandmother."

"No," Ruby snapped at her daughter. "Your grandmother and I were wrong to let things go on like we did. The Rubidoux have gone too far this time. Too damned far by a longshot and that hyped up little bitch is going to pay if it's the last thing I do in my life."

"But Daddy, Bernard, and Terry would still be alive if I hadn't ..." Julia couldn't finish the sentence for her tears.

"If you hadn't what, Priestess?" Ruby asked sternly. "If you hadn't insisted on saving this boy?" Ruby reached her hand out to Dalton, who stepped forward and took it. "You did the proper thing, Priestess. Never doubt your decisions where the coven is concerned. I taught you to be strong and decisive. Your father taught you to live by the Reade. He believed in the Laws that govern our kind. You must show our people back to the way. I allowed fear to sway my decision making as far as the Rubidoux were concerned, and now look where it's gotten us. They have broken the Laws that govern us. They've repeatedly done harm with their power, and that can no longer be tolerated. They must pay. You did the right thing in going to De la Croix." Ruby DuBois brought Dalton's hand to her lips and kissed it. "Do you think he'll respond?"

"He will after what we found out there today," Dalton said.

"What more has the evil little bitch done on top of everything else?" Ruby's eyes widened.

"We found thirteen more men in the Bayou that have been cursed with the *loup-garou* at Althea's bidding, and there were two women who've died since being cursed."

Ruby made the sign of the pentagram over her breast. "You can't be serious. Fifteen?"

"Yes, and one of them was Luther Rubidoux, her own cousin. It seems Althea promised him a place of power by her side if he'd help her poison his mother. He did, and then Althea accused him of murder before their coven and used the *loup-garou* on him as punishment. He was the first to be exiled to the bayou. Fourteen more followed. Six of them took their lives today when they found out there was no reversing the curse for them."

"And you've told Antoine all of this? Did he believe you?"

"I think he believed Luther," Julia said. "I made him confess his sins before he died, though I don't think he found absolution from Antoine De la Croix."

"I don't imagine he did." Ruby sighed. "Antoine and Eleanor had a *special* relationship if you know what I mean." Ruby raised an eyebrow. "When she got pregnant by him with Luther, her family arranged the marriage to her Rubidoux cousin in order for her to become Mother of the Rubidoux Coven."

"Ooo, ick," Julia said, scrunching her nose in disgust. "I always heard there was incest in that family, but ick."

"Yes, cousins have been marrying cousins in that line almost since the beginning to keep the bloodline pure. It was an old-world thing they couldn't put aside."

"The DuBois hasn't … uh, tried to keep the bloodline pure?" Julia stammered.

"Gracious, no." Ruby winked playfully at Dalton. "Now, I'm not saying some cousins haven't married cousins over the centuries, but none in recent memory that I'm aware of."

Dalton spoke up. "So, you're saying that Luther Rubidoux, who murdered his mother, is the son of this Antoine De la Croix, the Big Kahuna witch in the bayou?"

"Yes," said Ruby, "and I'm pretty certain the boy knew it. He was under the impression that the coven would make him High Priest of the Rubidoux because of it. I overheard him talking about it to Eleanor in the library once. He couldn't understand why the covens out here refused to have a male head when others like the De la Croix did." Ruby readjusted her blanket and reached for her plastic cup of water. "Eleanor tried to explain to him that the De la Croix practiced a different sort of magic, but he would have none of it. He ranted and raved about how Eleanor was stealing his birthright from him and his due dessert."

"Well," Dalton said, clearing his throat, "he certainly got his due desserts today. He died just like his mama."

"Nobody deserved to die like that," Julia sighed.

"He's better off than if Antoine De la Croix had gotten hold of him," Ruby said, and sipped from the straw in her pink plastic cup. "He's sure to have beheaded the boy for killing Eleanor, son."

"Did you just say he'd have been beheaded? What sort of justice system do you people have out here?"

"One that goes back centuries," Ruby told him. "And it's served us well. Very few break High Council Law."

"What do you think they'll do to Althea and her coven?" Dalton asked.

"Antoine will likely disband the Rubidoux, and have their properties confiscated. As disavowed and sanctioned, no coven will take them in, and they'll all be left to their own devices, without family to call upon in times of trouble. They will have to live as solitary practitioners and will not be able to start their own covens, at least not legal ones." Ruby sipped some more water. "I have no idea what De la Croix will do with Althea, but whatever it is, it won't be pretty. He'll want to make a spectacle of it, so everyone knows not to violate High Council Law while the De la Croix holds the position. I'm certain it will be especially harsh since the Rubidoux are right in De la Croix's backyard. He'll feel especially humiliated and make an example of her for the murder of Eleanor and likely his son as well."

"I imagine he'll hold her in the dungeons until The Witches' Ball in October," Julia said. "He'll undoubtedly do whatever he's going to do then when all the coven heads are there to witness it."

"Surely he won't hold a public execution in the middle of the Garden District." Dalton gasped. "Isn't that Ball open to the public?"

"There are two," Julia said, smiling weakly at her mother. "One is the public event where all the wanna-be posers show up in their Elvira wigs and Hogwarts cloaks. The other is held on the actual Solstice date for Samhain."

"Oh, I see." Dalton ran a hand through his hair. "I'm going to step out and get a Coke. Do either of you want anything?"

"No, but thank you, babe," Julia said. She watched him go and appreciated him for giving her some private time with her mother. "How are you, really, Mom?"

"I could be worse," Ruby DuBois admitted. "It was the Residual that killed your dad. He went to Bernard's body before I could get there, and by the time I reached them, Ben was gone." Tears ran down her face again. "The Residual was so strong. The casting must have been done right there on the spot, or nearby. How could they have known where Bernard and Terry, or any of you, were going to be?"

"Bernard probably told Althea," Julia said without thinking about her words.

"What are you talking about, daughter?"

"Bernard and Althea have been having an affair," Julia confessed to her wide-eyed mother. "Dalton saw them together last week holding hands and kissing in the parking lot at McDonald's. It was when Bernard was supposed to be in New Orleans on business."

"So that's who it was," Ruby sighed. "Terry knew he was seeing someone. It seems your brother had begun taking the dog out to the dog park at night after ten. A few weeks ago, he left the house, but forgot the damned dog."

"Oh, my." Julia rolled her eyes. How could her brother have been so foolish? "Bernard wasn't all that different from Luther Rubidoux."

"Excuse me?" Julia's mother questioned with a furrowed brow.

"Bernard got in my face the other night about how I was going to inherit everything. He wanted the house and the money from the DuBois Trust." Julia stared at her stricken mother, sadly. "I told him there was no money left in the DuBois Trust, but I don't think he believed me. I told him he could have the house if he wanted it. I didn't want it or the upkeep."

Ruby DuBois closed her eyes and bent her head. "I know. He came to your dad and me about a month ago, complaining that it

90

wasn't fair that the second-born female in the line should inherit everything when it was customary everyplace else that the oldest male should inherit it."

"I told him he could have the damned house." Julia interjected. "I just didn't know how he was going to keep it up on his Dollar General salary."

"Maybe he thought he could supplement it with Rubidoux money," Ruby said.

Julia's eyes went wide. "Oh my." She threw a hand over her mouth.

"What is it, Julia?" Ruby reached for her daughter's trembling hand.

"I know what happened," Julia stammered. "I know exactly what happened. Bernard must have told Althea the DuBois trust was empty." She shook her head and squeezed her mother's hand on the bed. "Althea was hoping to use the DuBois Trust to take care of *her* money problems. If Bernard told her he was as broke as her, she wouldn't need him any longer."

"The Rubidoux are broke?"

Julia nodded. "Luther said his mother had emptied their accounts years ago. He said Althea was very upset to find she'd become the head of a Coven deep in debt."

"A hundred years ago, both our Covens had many sources of income. We had investments in sugar plantations, the salt mines, and rice, but after the Depression a good bit of that dried up." Ruby shook her head sadly. "Our families owned interests in most of the industries in southern Louisiana, but poor management has cost us dearly."

Ruby took a deep breath. "Our names once meant something here, but now we're a laughing stock. People snicker at us behind our backs. People who once feared our power now laugh at us openly. The DuBois and Rubidoux are no longer names of nobility in the bayou. They're names joked about in bar rooms." Tears slid down Ruby's pale cheeks. "I'm sorry for leaving you nothing more than past glories and empty coffers, Julia."

"Mother, the power in our name has nothing to do with money. We're powerful because we're the DuBois. We're one of the most respected covens in the region."

Ruby huffed. "That and seven dollars will get you a fancy coffee at Starbucks. What do we have to offer these days? Mary and Peg sell herbs at the Farmers' market, and a few make and sell charms to shops in The Quarter. Franny reads Tarot in Jackson Square to make ends meet, but the DuBois are nothing like we once were."

13

B en, Bernard, and Terry DuBois were laid to rest in the
family crypt behind the DuBois mansion a few days after
the tragedy. It bolstered Ruby's spirits that so many from the
town were in attendance at the service held in the back garden
beneath blooming magnolia trees. None of the Rubidoux made
an appearance, but Antoine De la Croix showed up in his black
limousine along with an entourage of other coven leaders from
the region.

He took Ruby's hand in the receiving line and kissed it. "I am
so very sorry for your terrible losses, Mrs. DuBois."

"Thank you, Antoine. Thank you and the others for coming."
Ruby patted the big black man's smooth cheek before he moved
on to Julia.

"May we speak privately when things have settled here a bit,
Miss DuBois?"

"Of course, Mr. De la Croix. I'll meet with you in the study in
half an hour." Julia nodded toward a set of double doors at the
back of the room. "Please make yourself comfortable. There is
food and drink in the kitchen, or you may serve yourself from
the bar set up in the corner."

"You're very gracious." Antoine De la Croix dropped Julia's

hand, nodded to Dalton, who stood beside her and walked off toward the kitchen.

Julia whispered to Dalton, and he followed the big man into the room where Mary, Franny, and Peg were busy setting out food, stacking plates, and stirring tea.

"Miss Mary," Dalton touched the big woman on the shoulder, "Julia wanted me to ask you to bring a pitcher of tea and a plate of sandwiches with napkins and glasses into the study for her meeting with Mr. De la Croix and his friends."

"Sure, honey. No trouble at all. How are she and Miss Ruby holding up?"

"As well as can be expected, I suppose. How are the little guys doing?" Dalton glanced over at a nine year-old girl and a seven year-old boy dressed in their best clothes sitting at the nearby table. There was no missing the resemblance in the little girl to Terry, her mother.

"They're numb," Mary said. "Benny doesn't quite understand what's happened, but Melanie has picked up a bit of what's going on with the Rubidoux."

Dalton reached out with his senses and detected simmering rage coming from the petite blonde girl. The boy oozed confusion and overwhelming sadness. Dalton walked to the table with plates of peach pie in each hand. "Here you go." He set the plates in front of the children. "Miss Mary said to bring these to you."

Benny's eyes brightened in his freckled face. "Thanks, Dalton. I like pie."

Melanie pushed hers aside with a snarl. "I don't want no darned pie." Dalton knew she wanted to use words other than darned, and he couldn't blame her.

"It's all right, kiddo, I probably wouldn't want no damned pie neither," he said and winked.

It brought a reluctant smile to Melanie's lips, and she picked up her fork. "Thank you, Mr. La Pierre." Melanie returned his wink.

"You ever know anyone who died?" Benny asked in a soft voice. "I ain't never been to no funerals before."

"My sister died in a car accident a few years ago," Dalton said. "It's sad today, but every day the sadness gets a little farther away and a little easier to handle."

"Did you cry?" the little boy asked, stabbing at a stray peach slice that had escaped the crust.

"I still cry sometimes," Dalton admitted. "I'll hear a song on the truck's radio I know Marsha liked, and I'll just start ballin' like a baby. It's nothing to be ashamed of. It just means I loved her very much, and I miss her."

"Oh, OK," the boy said quietly, then popped the peach into his mouth.

"Did someone *kill* your sister?" Melanie asked with agitation Dalton could smell.

A surge of old guilt passed through Dalton, thinking about the accident that had taken Marsha's young life. "No, it was a car accident."

"Then you don't know how it feels," Melanie snapped, and Dalton smelled her anger again. Julia would need to talk to this child or get her some counseling with someone who understood the situation. There must be witch related psychotherapists. Kids in these families must have to deal with a lot of weird shit.

"No. I don't suppose I do. You should talk to your Aunt Julia. She just lost her dad *and* her brother. I know *she* knows how you're feeling."

"Yes, I do." Dalton heard Julia say from behind him. She went to her niece and kissed the top of her blond head. "We'll talk later, Mel. I need to steal Dalton away now to discuss some coven business."

"Is it about my mom and dad?" Benny asked with a mouth full of pie. "Are you gonna plan how to kill that Rubidoux bitch?" His face went pale when he looked up from his pie to see Dalton, Julia, and Melanie staring at him. "Well, it's what Mom called her."

95

"We'll talk later," Julia promised and took Dalton's hand. "Come on, babe. Let's go talk to the big kahuna."

Dalton followed Julia into a room with an ornate mahogany desk, floor to ceiling shelves filled with thick leather-bound books, a coffee table with a tray of sandwiches and a pitcher of iced tea, two wingback chairs upholstered in oxblood leather, and a matching couch. Antoine De la Croix sat in one of the chairs, holding a tall glass of tea with a wedge of lemon floating amongst the ice cubes. A sandwich and napkin rested upon his knee. A leggy blonde woman in black chiffon sat upon the couch with a brunette in a dark green pantsuit. Dalton supposed these were witch women from other covens in the region.

"Miss DuBois, you know Sandra Benet?" The brunette nodded. "And Laura Bourbon." The blonde nodded in turn.

"We're so sorry for your loss, Julia," said Sandra Benet, reaching for the pitcher of tea.

"And you are accusing the Rubidoux of all this?" Laura Bourbon asked skeptically. "What proof do you have? These are serious charges."

"They certainly are," Julia snapped. "This is Dalton La Pierre. Dalton, shake hands with everyone." She nodded her head slightly and winked.

Dalton offered his hand first to the brunette. She took it, gasped, and quickly released it as though she'd just touched a snake in her flower garden. The surly blonde did much the same, but Dalton refused to break contact. When he finally did, the woman wiped her hand on her skirt as if trying to rid herself of something slimy. Dalton then turned to Antoine De la Croix. The big man took his hand but showed no sign of detecting anything untoward.

"If you need any further convincing, there are seven men in a glen up the Vermillion in the same condition." Julia poured two glasses of sweet tea and handed one to Dalton. He could smelll her rage building through her grief. "There were six others, but they killed themselves when they were told we could not reverse their conditions. One of them was Luther Rubidoux, and he made his admissions to Mr. De la Croix over the phone." Julia glanced at the big man in his chair, sipping tea. "I'm sorry for *your* loss as well." Julia let him know she knew his secret with those words. Dalton sensed no grief in the man, only a hint of agitation.

"Is this true, Antoine? I thought the boy had disappeared after losing his mother." Laura Bourbon sipped her tea.

"He disappeared into the bayou because Althea Rubidoux cursed him with the loup-garou." Julia snarled. "He and twelve others have been hiding out there away from civilization, so they wouldn't take the chance of killing anyone. They hid themselves away, protecting our secrets as well as theirs. Althea Rubidoux has endangered all of us, and when my coven attempted to collect the items needed to reverse the curse, she sent people out to attack and kill us. Luther said he heard some of them saying she'd given them a shoot-to-kill order. Rubidoux magic killed my brother and sister-in-law, and then my father, when he came in contact with the Residual. My father was one of the strongest proponents of the Reade, and he was killed by someone breaking it." Julia shook her head in frustration.

"The Reade is passé," the blonde said and tore off a bit of sandwich. "I'll not condemn someone for going against that."

"It's all right to break one law, but not another?" Julia turned to De la Croix. "Since when are we allowed to pick and choose which Council Laws we want to follow or disavow? The Reade goes back to our very roots. It has ever been our one moral compass. If we have elected to throw it out the window, we are doomed as a society. We may as well come out of the shadows and offer up our services to the highest bidder, creating armies of *loup-garou* and *Strega*.

"Now Miss DuBois," De la Croix interrupted, "let's not get carried away. Many have suggested in Council that we amend the Reade. None of our coffers are as full as they once were, and if we went out into the world with our arcane knowledge, we would all be the better for it. The DuBois, with their healing abilities, could become notable once more. Other covens have honed skills in other useful areas."

"I can't believe I'm hearing this. Are you actually considering bringing our abilities out into the open? What do you think will happen when governments realize what we can do? They will enslave us to do their bidding."

"And how would they control us, DuBois? They can't possibly know how," Laura Bourbon spat.

"If you're willing to sell our secrets, how long do you think it would take until another is willing to give up other secrets if the price were right. You could find yourself bound in lead and stripped of your powers, and chained to some old man's bed as a plaything." Julia shook her head, and Dalton could smell her fear and disgust. "You're all fools if you don't think our enemies can't discover our weaknesses. There are libraries out there with that information, not to mention others greedy enough to give it up for a price. Althea Rubidoux would be one of the first in line to sell out the High Council if she thought it would refill her bank account. I, for one, am not willing to take that chance."

"You are absolutely correct about Althea Rubidoux and her coven," De la Croix said. "As we speak, she and her people are being taken into custody by High Council Authorities. They will be remanded to high-security facilities until a full Council can be gathered. We will expect you and your mother to give testimony." De la Croix studied Dalton momentarily. "Where are you planning to conduct the ritual to counter the *loup-garou?*"

"As we have eight subjects to work on, we thought we should perform the ritual out at the glen where the other men have been living. It is secluded and far from inhabited areas."

"Why not simply shoot them all and be done with it?" Laura Bourbon asked smugly. "Perform the ritual on your pup here," she nodded to Dalton, "but the others are of no real consequence."

"Laura, Sylvia would be appalled to hear you say such a

thing." Dalton hadn't heard or sensed Ruby DuBois slip into the room. "Your mother was as staunch a proponent of the Reade as my Ben, and she'd have been one of the first to add her gift to the Circle to save these poor cursed souls. Sandra, I haven't heard from you. What is the stand of the Benet Coven in these matters?"

Sandra Benet stood and adjusted her green silk suit. She ignored Laura Bourbon's stare and looked directly at the big black man sipping his tea. "The Benet will stand with the Reade. We will also be here with our full Circle to add our strength to the DuBois in reversing this atrocity."

"Thank you, Sandra." Ruby walked to the woman and hugged her. "Julia will let you know what else we might need in the way of herbs and other items for the ritual. The Rubidoux attacked several of our teams, and not everything we needed could be acquired.

"Just let me know what you need. We have ample stores and people eager to assist. I assume you'll need Wolf's bane and colloidal silver for the binding."

"We have plenty of Wolf's bane, but we could use more colloidal silver," Julia told her with a smile. "Everyone will be meeting at the docks on the Vermillion at three in the afternoon of the full moon, to head upriver."

"We'll be ferrying ATVs up there ahead of time, so we won't have to walk everything and everyone in. It's a long trek back there on foot," Dalton added.

"It sounds as though you've been giving this some serious planning," Laura scoffed. "My dear mother's feelings aside, I still think it's a waste of time and resources. Shoot them all and be done with them. We don't need a bunch of loose lips out there telling tales."

"And who do you think would believe them? The National Enquirer?" Dalton asked. "I think you're pretty safe on that account."

"You could very well be correct," De la Croix said. "The De la

Croix Coven and the Council will back this ritual. We, too, will add our power to this Circle."

"Thank you, Mr. De la Croix," Dalton said. "I appreciate it, and I'm certain the other aflicted men will as well."

De la Croix stood and shook Dalton's hand. "You're very welcome, Mr. La Pierre. If you would be willing, I'd like you to speak with one of my associates about your enhanced senses. My son said something to me about it, and I'd like to get some documentation from someone with first-hand knowledge. If you would be willing, of course."

Dalton looked at Julia, and she nodded slightly. "I suppose if it would be for the sake of knowledge, I'm game."

"Thank you, Mr. La Pierre. I will be in touch after the ritual." He turned to Julia. "Thank you for bringing this atrocity to my attention, and I'm sorry for the losses you and your family have suffered because of it." He then turned to Ruby DuBois. "Ruby, I am so very sorry for your loss."

"Thank you, Antoine. I'm sorry for your losses as well. I know Eleanor was very dear to you, and I'm sorry to hear how terribly she actually died. We were all under the impression she'd died of complications of the flu."

"As did I. Luther refused an autopsy, of course, and I had no authority. I have since had her body exhumed, and it was as Luther admitted. The physicians found evidence of the poison in her poor body." Antoine De la Croix sighed, and Dalton sensed fury in the man. "Althea Rubidoux and her coven will be dealt with harshly."

# 14

Julia kissed her mother then walked with Dalton to her car. "I'm so ready to go home," she said as she slid into the passenger seat and fastened her seatbelt.

"Me too, Jules." He started the car and shifted into reverse. "Your mom seemed better tonight after meeting with De la Croix and his chippies."

"She's better because of having Benny and Melanie here. She has them in my and Bernard's old rooms. It will be good for all of them."

"Melanie is full of rage," Dalton said as he pulled out onto the road. "You might want to have her talk to somebody."

"Aren't *you* full of rage?" Julia snapped. "I'm sure she is. Things will settle down soon. Once we get all of this business taken care of, I'll see about having her talk to someone. There's a woman in New Orleans from one of the covens who deals with our children and the problems specific to them."

"I'm sorry, Jules. This is all my fault."

"It is *not* your fault. This is on Althea and nobody else."

They rode in silence for the rest of the journey home. Dalton parked the car and opened the door. He didn't know what to say. Julia jumped down his throat, no matter what he said. He knew she must be exhausted and emotionally drained. They'd buried her father, brother, and sister-in-law that morning. Her mother, still weak from her emotional collapse, now had to deal with two orphaned grandchildren in that big, old house. Mary and Hal had moved in to help, but Dalton didn't know how the older woman would handle it.

Dalton followed Julia up the stairs and waited for her to unlock the door. Inside, she tossed her purse onto the couch and slipped her keys onto the hook by the door. He took Julia's petite body into his arms and held her. He felt her relax in his embrace and smelled the tension leaving her body. Dalton lifted her chin, bent down, and kissed her. The kiss was soft and sweet in the beginning but soon built to something more.

Juiia, a strong empath, sensed his need and wanted to do what she could to quell his need. She leaned into the kiss and allowed herself to be carried into the need as well. The day had been trying and perhaps what she needed was the release of her tension with sex.

Their tongues found one another's, and Dalton could taste her sweet saltiness. The taste and smell of her ignited a fire in Dalton's groin that he couldn't ignore. He lifted Julia into his arms and carried her into the bedroom.

Dalton laid her upon the unmade bed with her head resting upon the rumpled pillows. He stripped off his shirt and kicked off his loafers. Julia unbuttoned her dress and slipped it from her shoulders. She pushed it down past her hips and kicked it to the foot of the bed. Watching her undress excited Dalton, and when he pushed down his underwear, his erection sprang out hard and ready. Hungry for her, Dalton pulled Julia's bra down to expose her erect pink nipples, and he fell upon her breast, sucking savagely at the hard nuggets of flesh.

"Oh, yes, Dalton. Suck harder and bite. Ahhh, yes, that's it. You do that so nice." Julia moaned and thrashed under his body.

He could smell her desire for him. After pinching her nipple, Dalton took his hand away to slide down the smooth skin of her belly, and into the mound of course hair above her vagina. He used a finger to find her clit and flicked it softly before sliding into her, massaging the clit into an engorged mound of throbbing tissue. Julia moaned and arched her back to meet the attentions of his finger playing inside her.

"Fuck me, babe," Julia moaned, spreading her legs wider.

The smell of her sex drove Dalton into a mad frenzy of need. Without regard for her, Dalton grabbed Julia's hips and flipped her over onto her belly. He yanked her hips up to meet his stiff cock and shoved into her from behind. On his knees, Dalton held onto Julia's tender ass cheeks and pummeled her hot wet crevasse with his throbbing cock. All he cared about was satisfying his lust for her. His cock throbbed inside her. With each long stroke, all he could think about was planting his seed inside *his* female. Her vagina was his playground, and he pounded into it.

Julia met his thrusts and groaned pleasurably, but Dalton's pleasure came from possessing her. She was his, and he would have her. Dalton heard Julia scream his name, and her muscles contracted around his cock as her orgasm exploded. Those contractions brought about his orgasm, and he howled with delight as his seed flooded into her, *his* woman.

Dalton's cock wilted out of her, and Julia rolled onto her back to look up into his eyes. He leered down at her.

"Dalton?" he heard Julia saying his name, but he was far away, caught in the after-effects of their coupling. He stared down at her and wanted her again. "Dalton!" He heard her, but he didn't hear her. Something kept him from saying what he wanted to say to her. Other words came instead. Words other than his.

"Did you like that, you sticky little cunt? Do you like it when he shoves it in you like the dog he is now? Look into the mutt's eyes, DuBois. He's mine. I can feel it when he cums in you, and it feels good. I can make his cock hard again, and we can fuck your cunt all night, DuBois."

"Dalton!" Julia screamed. She wrenched her hand free of his and slapped him. "Come back, Dalton. Break free of her!" Julia slapped him again.

His cock was hard again, and Dalton could smell Julia's wet musky sex. It smelled of his seed, but it smelled of her creamy wetness too. He wanted it again. He didn't smell her need for him this time, though. He smelled fear and anger. Why was she angry?

"Dalton, come back," Julia begged.

His cock wilted, and Dalton's head spun. "What the fuck?" He sat on his knees, straddling Julia in her bed. Her eyes glared back at him with fear and distrust. Dalton rolled off Julia's body and onto the pillows beside her. "What just happened, Jules? My head is pounding." He rubbed at his eyes to clear the stabbing pain behind them.

"I think Althea Rubidoux just screwed me."

"What?" Dalton bolted upright beside her. "What did you just say?"

Julia grabbed some tissues from the box on her bedside table and wiped between her legs. "I think Althea was in possession of you while we ... while we just screwed. What do you remember?"

"I remember carrying you into the bedroom. I remember wanting you really bad. I could smell you. You wanted me, and I wanted you more because of it." Dalton shook his head and rubbed at the pain behind his eyes again. "I took you from behind. I had to have you like that." Dalton gasped. "I'm sorry, Jules. Did I hurt you?"

"No, but it wasn't just you. Althea was in there. Do you remember talking to me?"

"I remember *wanting* to talk to you, but my words wouldn't come. Did I call you a cunt?" Dalton asked with self-loathing.

"You didn't, but *she* did."

"What the hell, Jules? I don't understand."

MOON OF THE WITCH

"I don't understand exactly, either, babe," Julia sighed and took his hand, "but I'm gonna figure it out."

"Thanks, Jules. I'm really sorry about all of this. I wish I understood what's going on."

"It's not you, babe. It's her," Julia told him. "Somehow, she's made a psychic connection with you and can take control. When you're in that wolfy state, I think it's easier for her." Julia kissed his mouth. "I'm going to talk to my mom about it tomorrow and see if I can find anything in the Grimoire about it. Maybe there's some way we can use it against her."

Julia's phone chimed from her purse in the living room. She threw her legs over the edge of the bed and stood. "I'd better get that. It might be important."

Dalton watched her walk naked from the bedroom. His head still throbbed, but he doubted aspirin would help with *this* headache. Julia came back into the bedroom with her phone at her ear. "I'll look for that in the Grimoire. Thanks." She dropped the phone onto the bedside table.

"What's up?" Dalton asked, pulling the sheet up over his naked body.

"That was Antoine. His people have rounded up several of the Rubidoux from the compound on the island, but Althea wasn't with them." Julia picked up her dress from the bottom of the bed, shook it out, and hung it back in her wardrobe. She picked up her bra and pantyhose and tossed them into her hamper before slipping back into the bed next to Dalton.

"They're still looking for her. I told him about what happened, and he told me what to look for in the Grimoire. He says there's a way to take control of her when she's in control of you, but it's tricky." Julia stretched, then turned off the lamp on the table next to her. "I'll study what I can find and ask Mom what she knows about it. Antoine said it's very dark magic. Mom might not know anything about it, but he thought it should be mentioned in our Grimoire someplace. Even though the DuBois don't practice dark magic, we need to have the means to counter it."

"Sounds like a lot of work." Dalton yawned. "How long did you take off from the bank?"

"I had two weeks' vacation time coming and a week for bereavement. Three weeks gives me more than enough time to deal and prepare for the ritual next week."

"Maybe after the ritual, we can run down to the islands for a few days," Dalton suggested. "You deserve some downtime. A friend of mine runs a hotel on the beach in Negril."

"That sounds divine even if it *is* still hurricane season." Julia rolled over and kissed Dalton's cheek.

15

---

J ulia made arrangements for everything they'd need for the ritual, as well as arrangements to house all the other coven members coming in to add their strength to the Circle. As things stood, it looked as though they would have enough people to prepare four full circles. Two men could be worked on in each of the four. They would place the men who'd been through the most changes in the same circle. Their curses would take the most power to reverse, and Julia planned to have that particular circle officiated by Antoine De la Croix, by far the most powerful witch of them all.

A dozen different ATVs were being shuttled to the spot on the Vermillion River closest to the Glen, where the afflicted men resided. Coven members gathered and delivered bags of groceries, clothing, and toiletries for the men since their discovery. Julia didn't know how they'd gotten by out there for so long with little to no assistance from Althea and her coven. Larry had told Julia and Dalton that supplies were sometimes left by the river, but those deliveries had become fewer and farther between as time went by. She hoped her care packages eased their suffering. A few had been able to use her phone to contact their family with only minimal sickness from the poison after the poisoned men had used it to say their goodbyes.

Julia had no idea what excuses they'd given to explain their lengthy absences, but she was sure hearts had been eased on both sides. Julia prayed they would be able to reverse all the cursed to their normal selves, but she seriously doubted any of them would ever feel normal again.

Althea Rubidoux had seemingly disappeared from the island in the Black Bayou and St. Elizabeth. Her Mercedes had disappeared from its parking place at the Rubidoux dock, and nobody had seen it around town. For all intents and purposes, Althea and the Rubidoux Coven were no more. The island stood empty of human life. Some locals friendly with the family had removed pets and livestock from the island, and Julia suspected that soon the place would be stripped of anything of value. While the Rubidoux had been feared a century ago, their reputation had dwindled to no more than scary stories told by old folks. Some might avoid the island for fear of ghosts, but not for fear of non-existent witches. They must have lowered their wards from the place when they'd left the island. Possibly the De la Croix had destroyed them before their invasion.

Julia had searched the Grimoire for the spell to take control of Althea while she possessed Dalton but could find none. She took the big book with her to visit her mother. Melanie and Benny had returned to school after the funerals and seemed to be adjusting to their new surroundings and circumstances.

"Hey, Mom," Julia said upon entering the kitchen by way of the open patio doors. "You downstairs?"

"I'll be down in a minute, sweetheart. There's still coffee in the pot and some rolls on the counter."

Julia poured a cup of coffee but passed on the roll. Ruby DuBois came into the kitchen carrying a plastic laundry basket filled with pink and blue bedsheets. Julia smiled, thinking back to her childhood. Today was Tuesday and Tuesday had always been sheet changing day in the DuBois house.

"Can't Melanie pull the sheets off those beds before leaving for school? I always did."

Ruby DuBois smiled at her daughter. "It's a little too soon for hard labor, don't you think? I'll ease them into it." Ruby stopped when she saw the Grimoire set upon her kitchen table. "Do you need help with the *loup-garou?*"

"No, it's something else." Julia picked up her coffee cup and went on to explain what had happened with Dalton and how Antoine De la Croix had told her there should be something about it in her Grimoire.

"Unfortunately," Ruby said, dropping the basket onto the floor of the laundry room. "That book doesn't contain the answers to everything.

"Oh," Julia said sadly. "But I can't have that bitch just popping in every time Dalton and I want to have sex."

"I can certainly see where that would be an annoyance." Ruby poured a fresh cup of coffee and joined Julia. She took the book Julia had opened and began leafing through the stiff pages of painted parchment. "I've never dealt with anything like it, but I think this is what you're looking for. It can be tricky and will drain you. I don't know that I'd want to attempt it without a really strong Second standing by." She pushed the book to Julia who scanned the translation on the page.

"This doesn't sound so complicated. Daddy used to put thoughts into my head and have me reply without speaking out loud all the time. I don't have the gift of telepathy as strong as he did, but I can certainly do *this.*"

"I'd forgotten he practiced with you. You should cultivate it. I know some can't receive but I'm certain many of the other DuBois and Benet do. The next time you're around them, reach out. You might be surprised." Ruby smiled and touched Julia's hand. "Evidently your boy can. Daddy said he spoke to him and Dalton heard what he said. He told me Dalton was projecting clearly too, but that may be a side-effect of the *loup-garou.* Didn't you say his other senses have become enhanced?"

"Yes. His sense of smell and hearing are much improved, and he can pick up on moods. He says he can smell them. I don't quite get that, but it's what he says. Says he can *smell* anger or fear."

"He may be an empath and the wolf senses have brought it to the surface. He says he smells it because his enhanced nose is picking up the scents our bodies give off when frightened or angry. It may be something he won't completely lose when we lift the *loup-garou*."

"That would be handy," Julia sighed out. "I could use a strong empath in the coven now that Terry's gone."

"An empath who's also a telepath would be a true gift from the Goddess. Is your Dalton open to joining and working with us?"

"After all of this, I don't think it would be hard to talk him into it. If I can prove to him that he has certain natural abilities, I'm sure he'll join us. All of his skepticism has been washed away already."

"He's an open-minded young man and if you can develop his natural gifts, he can become an asset to you in more than just the bedroom." Ruby laughed.

"Speaking of assets and natural gifts, have you tested the children at all yet?"

"You are their Priestess," Ruby said without meeting Julia's eyes. "It is your place."

"And you are their grandmother who *was* our Priestess. If anyone should test them, it should be you." Julia smiled at her beaming mother across the table. "Come on, Mom, out with it."

"Both have your father's gift of telepathy. I hear them talking all the time." Ruby gave her daughter a mischievous grin. "I'll wait for a while before I let them know I can hear them, too. Melanie has a bit of her mother's empathy, but it's not as strong as Terry's was. She senses the creatures around her and picks up on emotions like your Dalton. She will be a very effective Priestess someday if she ever learns to keep her emotions from controlling her. Perhaps Dalton can help her with that if lifting the *loup-garou* doesn't destroy his abilities in that regard. Benny is very taken with Dalton, by the way, and Melanie thinks he's *cute.*"

"He's quite fond of them both," Julia admitted, "and he's worried about Melanie's rage. He thinks I should take her to see Miss Amanda in New Orleans."

"I've been thinking about that. It might do Mel some good and help her work through her grief."

"That would be the only thing to take her for. She's been to her first moon circle and understands about our family. Growing up surrounded by it, she shouldn't have the problems some coven parents have explaining the need for secrecy. I just hate it that her parents died at the hands of another coven. I don't want it in her head this early that magic can be used to kill."

"You're twenty-eight and I don't want it in your head, either."

Julia laughed, picked up her Grimoire, and kissed her mother. "Bye, Mom. Next Wednesday can't get here soon enough."

"I know, sweetheart. Study that incantation until you have it put to memory. You can't afford to miss a syllable."

"I've been studying," Julia said. "If I were in the right phase of the moon, Dalton would be cured already."

"Be careful of that." Ruby called after her. "I caused my roses to bloom out of season once. They were never right after that."

"Thanks, Mom. I'll be careful." Feeling light-hearted, Julia got into her car and drove toward home. As she passed the docks, Julia was stunned to see Althea Rubidoux's black Mercedes sitting in its regular spot. Could she actually be out on the island? Julia turned her car around and parked in a shady spot with a clear view of the expensive automobile. A thick layer of dust attested to the car's neglect since its owner had gone into hiding.

Julia sat for less than an hour before she heard the drone of an outboard motor. She squinted her eyes to look out over the bayou and see a small boat headed to the docks from Rubidoux Island. In fifteen more minutes Althea Rubidoux lifted a heavy wooden chest onto the dock from the swaying boat. As Althea began to climb from the boat, Julia stepped out of her car and slammed the door. On high alert, Althea dropped back into the concealing boat, but saw the little redhead. Julia moved swiftly toward the dock, reaching it before Althea had climbed back up completely and regained her footing upon the wooden planking.

"You're here without your hound?" Althea laughed.

Julia stormed down the dock and headed directly to the Rubidoux Ritual Chest. Too late, Althea realized Julia's intent. Before the tall, thin woman could grab it, Julia used her momentum to push the chest off the end of the dock to sink into the muddy water of Black Bayou.

"You bitch," Althea screamed, grabbing for the precious box of ceremonial items dear to the former High Priestess of the Rubidoux Coven. "That chest and my Grimoire have been with the Rubidoux since France. Go down and get it." She grabbed onto Julia and tried to push her off the dock to follow the sunken box.

Julia gathered power from around her, drawing from every living thing in her midst. She batted Althea's hands away with ease. "There are no Rubidoux any longer, Althea," Julia stormed. "You are nameless and without a coven. When the De la Croix finds you, you'll join the others in the dungeons to await your trials. The murder of your High Priestess will probably earn you a beheading and if not that, then for the poor souls you cast the *loup-garou* upon.

"You have no proof I had anything to do with Eleanor's death. She was an old woman who caught the flu and died. That's all."

"That's not what Luther said." Julia taunted. Was it possible Althea didn't know they'd found Luther and the others?

"What do you know of Luther Rubidoux? He ran off after his wretched mother died."

"Yes, ran off to a glen near the Vermillion to make the change every month."

"Luther wanted to head a coven." Althea rolled her eyes and smirked. "Now he has one. He can be the top-dog he always dreamed of being." Althea began laughing maniacally.

"Luther is dead, Althea. He and five of the others you cursed took their lives rather than go on living as they had."

"If Luther is dead, he's of no consequence to me. Dead men tell no tales, DuBois."

"Luther told his tales before he died."

"To whom? You and your hound? Don't make me laugh."

"No, Althea, he told his father."

"Luther's father has been dead for twenty years."

"Not his Rubidoux step-father, Althea. He told his real father, Antoine De la Croix. Luther confessed everything before he died to De la Croix." Julia watched Althea's beautiful face turn to one of surprise, then horror. "You mean you didn't know Antoine De la Croix was Eleanor's lover and Luther's father? You were the High Priestess of the Rubidoux. How could you not have known such an important family fact?"

"But my mother always said Antoine was the father of a future power of the Rubidoux. I thought she meant me. I thought Antoine De la Croix was *my* father. How could she have thought Luther would be a power of the Rubidoux? He was a simpering little fool."

"Althea, your mama may have screwed every cock in the Parish, but she never slept with Antoine De la Croix. He had better taste than that. Antoine loved Eleanor and he knows you killed her with Pixie Arrow poison in a box of chocolates."

"Antoine's not my father?" Althea asked, looking thunderstruck. "He knows about Eleanor? How could he know for certain?"

"Because he had her body exhumed and an autopsy

113

performed. He knows she was poisoned and he knows with what."

"I told that fool Luther to have the bitch cremated," Althea spat.

"Antoine would not have allowed that. She was a Priestess of the Rubidoux and entitled to her place of honor in the family crypt."

"I'm going to kill you, Julia DuBois," Althea suddenly screamed. "You stole my man from me. I cursed him, but I'm going to *kill* you."

"Why did you kill my brother, Althea? Bernard always wanted peace between our families. He even took your side about using the *loup-garou* on Dalton. Why did you have to kill him?"

"Bernard was a stupid fool," Althea sneered. "After Luther told me the Rubidoux family was in ruins, I thought to use Bernard and the DuBois trust. I had your silly brother certain he was in love with me. I had him talked into leaving that silly little cow he married. Then he told me the DuBois was in no better shape than we were.

"Your brother was a dynamo in bed, so I thought I'd hang on to him for that." Althea cackled. "He even told me about your silly plan to reverse Dalton's curse and where your little hunting parties would be." Althea took a step toward Julia with a smile on her unblemished face. "I thought I'd go and give sweet little Terry and maybe even Bernard a few stings while they gathered your precious nectar."

Althea's face suddenly darkened and her smile turned into a hideous thin line of rage "I watched them from the barn. Terry spread a blanket on the grass and took out wine. They gathered nectar for a while, but then she stripped and lured him back to the blanket. I couldn't believe my eyes when the fool got undressed."

Althea shook her head. The wind off the bayou blew her loose coils of black hair. To Julia they looked like water moccasins twining around Althea's honey-colored neck. "I couldn't believe he was going to fuck her after he'd just been with me the night before. I stirred up the bees and called in as many as I could." Althea laughed again. "You should have seen the idiot trying to shield Terry from the bees with his body." Julia watched Althea roll her big brown eyes. "The big stupid fuck."

Julia had heard enough. She doubled up her fist and with all the power she'd called to her, punched Althea in her laughing mouth. Julia's punch connected with such force it sent Althea flying off the end of the dock to join the Rubidoux chest at the bottom of the Black Bayou.

With a sense of deep satisfaction, Julia returned to her car, got in, and drove home. The radio was playing her favorite song: "Witchy Woman."

## 16

The week passed slowly for Dalton. He'd laughed when Julia had told him about her encounter with Althea on the dock. He could almost see Althea tumbling off the end, ruining her designer clothes in the muck of the bayou.

He and Julia had made love that night, certain Althea would be in no condition to intrude upon them.

Julia talked with him about her father and Terry's psychic abilities. Dalton knew what telepathy was, but Julia had to explain empathy in the paranormal sense of the word.

"Get it?" she'd asked and met him with a broad smile when he'd looked up to answer her question. "Do you hear me?"

"Of course I ..." he stared wide-eyed and his mouth fell open. *"Did you just talk into my head?"* Dalton asked without speaking.

Julia threw her arms around Dalton's neck. "Mom was right. You can project *and* receive thoughts. You're a gifted telepath, Dalton."

"Have I always been this way or is it the wolfy thing?" They'd begun using the euphemism for his curse. They both thought it sounded less Sci-Fi than werewolf or *loup-garou* when conversing where others might overhear.

"I'd have to say you've probably always possessed the ability and the curse has enhanced it like your senses of smell and hearing."

"And will it go away after the curse is lifted?"

Julia shrugged her shoulders. "It may, but now that you know you have the ability, I think we can exercise it. My dad used to do it with me when I was little. We'd talk to one another even when I was upstairs in my room and him downstairs or outside. Mom could hear us so we really couldn't get away with anything. She has the natural ability to receive thoughts, but not the ability to project."

Dalton's face darkened. "Is it this natural ability that allows Althea to intrude in my mind?"

"Yes, but it's your natural ability that's going to help us use it against her if she pops in again."

"I don't know that I want her popping in again. I don't like being out of control and when she's in here," Dalton said, pointing toward his head, "I don't know exactly what's happening. She can see through my eyes and talk through my mouth. For god's sake, Jules, she can even feel it when I cum."

"I know, babe, but now that you know how it feels when she's trying to get in, you can turn it around on Althea and see through *her* eyes. Now that you know you have the ability, you can use it against her."

"I don't know I just don't know." Dalton shook his head slowly. He didn't know what to think about this telepathy thing. Maybe Jules had a point? Maybe if they practiced this thing he could pull one over on Althea, but he didn't know. He could honestly say he was afraid of Althea and her power. Now that he'd seen real magic in action and the results, Dalton didn't know if he really wanted to mess with her. Julia assured him that without her coven and her ritual items, Althea's power would be greatly diminished.

"This will all be over tomorrow, Dalton. After that, any connection she might have with you will be severed, and I'll teach you how to know if she's trying to get back in." Julia wrapped her arms around his neck and kissed him. "Let's go to bed, babe."

"One last night with the wolf?" Dalton teased and returned her kiss. He could smell her desire and the scent of her sex. He licked his lips. There were certain aspects of this wolfy thing Dalton was going to miss.

"Yeah, right," Julia said with a giggle and kissed him again. "Your kisses are still the same. Those haven't changed and the sex is the same except when the bitch is in your head." Julia took his hand. "Come on. Tomorrow's gonna be a busy day and we won't have time to enjoy one another." She began dragging Dalton toward the bedroom.

"OK, OK. I give."

Julia turned and winked. "Yes, you certainly will." She kicked her shoes under the edge of her bed and pulled her tank top off, releasing her ample breasts.

"You're a wicked woman." Dalton unbuckled his belt and dropped his jeans to the floor. He had his t-shirt around his head when he felt his briefs being yanked down over his behind. His erection slowed it, but Julia soon had them down and around his feet. He stepped out of the briefs tangled around his ankles and turned to the bed. Julia sprawled naked across the rumpled blankets with a smile on her lips. She parted them and took his cock into her mouth. "Oh, Jules, that feels incredible, but I want to be in you tonight."

Julia released his erection and rolled onto her back as she scooted up onto the pillows. She raised her arms, inviting Dalton to her. "Come on, babe. I want you, too."

Dalton stroked his throbbing cock as he straddled Julia's pale, naked body. The musky scent of her hot sex and her yearning for his attentions overwhelmed Dalton's senses. He ran his strong hands up her torso until he got to her heavy breasts. He kneaded both of them and began pinching her nipples between his thumb and forefingers. Dalton's cock throbbed with more intensity as he heard each of Julia's gasps of pleasure. He pinched and rolled them harder.

Julia moaned, "Oh, babe, you know just what I like." Sweat began to glisten upon her thin body and Dalton could smell her need for him. Her excitement ignited him and he had to have her. "Ahhh, yes," she said as his cock entered her. "Give it to me good." Julia met his thrusts and used her vaginal muscles to grip and release his hard cock as it slid in and out of her hot wetness, teasing her engorged clit. Julia's sharp, unpainted fingernails dug into Dalton's muscular back, but he didn't care. What she was doing to his cock was driving him to an orgasm. He wanted to hold back until Julia had hers, so he slowed his thrusts.

Dalton bent and sucked a nipple between his teeth. He drew his attention to the hard pink mound of flesh that would hasten her climax. He brushed it with his tongue between soft bites. "Oh my god, Dalton," Julia gasped, "Oh my god." Her vaginal muscles contracted hard upon his cock with her orgasm and Dalton quickened his pace once more.

"Ahhh, yes, yes," he howled as his orgasm burst from his pulsing erection. Dalton gave her another kiss before rolling off her sweat-damp body. He lay panting upon the pillows beside her. "That was great, Jules, and it was all me."

"Yes, it was." Julia rested beside him. "It was all you and you're all mine."

"I love you, Jules," Dalton said softly into the darkness around him. He heard her take in a sharp breath.

"I love you too, Dalton. I really do. If we can't lift the curse tomorrow and we have to take you to the glen once a month for the change, I'll still love you. I'll love you no matter what."

Dalton could smell the truth in her words. "Thanks, Jules, but you think it's gonna work, don't you?"

"Yes, babe, I absolutely do. You above all the others have the best chance, because you've never turned except for the cursing itself." Julia rolled over and put her arm reassuringly across Dalton's broad chest. "You I'm certain we can save, but we're gonna do our best to save the others, too. I know that ritual backward and forward, Mary has all the ingredients for the binding and with all the covens there, we'll have plenty of power."

Dalton tossed and turned for a while with worry, but when he heard Julia's soft, even breaths, he relaxed. If she could calm herself and sleep, so could he. He knew he needed to rest. Jules had said the next day would be taxing and Dalton had smelled the truth in her words. This lie detecting skill was going to be missed, if nothing else.

## 17

The sun, filtering through her lace curtains, woke Julia. She took a deep breath and her nose filled with the scents of frying bacon and coffee. She rolled to find Dalton's side of the bed empty. Remembering what lay ahead of her today, Julia swung her legs over the side of her bed and stood. She stretched and made her way to the bathroom. A damp towel hung over the shower rod. As she exited the bathroom, she wrapped herself in her robe, then trudged into the kitchen.

Julia stopped short of the kitchen when she saw Dalton, dressed in jeans and a t-shirt, standing over the range. Her heart skipped a beat when she remembered the horrific nightmare of him transformed into the *loup-garou*.

*Maybe I'm still asleep and when I call his name, it's not going to be Dalton, but that terrible, furry beast?*

She took a deep breath and walked into the kitchen. "It smells good in here, babe." Julia saw his half empty coffee cup on the table and the folded newspaper. "What time did you get up?" She glanced at the digital clock as she passed the microwave and saw that it read seven-twenty-five.

"I've been up a couple of hours. I woke up and had to pee, so I just stayed up. I was wide awake." Dalton turned and Julia's mind eased as he set a cup of black coffee in front of her. "I had a shower and heard the paper hit the porch, so I made some coffee."

"Thanks." Julia picked up the cup and sipped the hot brew. She was certain he could detect her fear as she'd come into the room. "Anything interesting in the paper?"

"They found Norm Potete's body floating in Black Bayou yesterday," Dalton said, sadly. "I wonder what they did with the others."

"Probably did away with all of them in water, so they'd be found eventually. Maybe not Luther's, but I'm sure they wanted the other mens' families to have bodies to bury."

"You're probably right." Dalton picked up his cold cup of coffee and added some fresh from the pot to warm it before taking a seat across from her. "What's the day going to look like? I left a note on the Garage that I'm going to be off for a day or two."

"I'm going to take a bath with ritual oils this morning since I won't have time or facilities before the ceremony. I'll take some of the oils with me to anoint myself just before." She had to remind herself that Dalton had never experienced a Full Moon Circle of the Coven before. He had no idea about cleansing baths or ritual oils. This was all still new to him.

"Do I need to take one too?"

"No," Julia said with a smile. "We'll anoint you with the necessary oils after we've bound you and the others with the Wolf's Bane and the colloidal silver mixture."

"Isn't Wolf's Bane a poison?" Dalton took a long drink of his coffee, then rose as the toast popped up.

"It is in large doses. This potion will keep all y'all from going into the change when the moon rises. We can't begin the ritual until a certain point during the moon's passage across the sky, and if you're not bound, you'd make the change and probably kill us all."

Dalton sat a plate of bacon onto the table along with smaller

MOON OF THE WITCH

plates holding slices of warm buttered toast. "I thought we might need some protein to start our day. I know you said you're sure this is going to work, but I can smell your fear, Jules," Dalton said as he sat again. "Are you gonna have a gun out there with silver bullets in case it doesn't?"

"The binding should be more than enough to keep all of you under control," Julia assured him.

"If this potion works to keep you from making the change, why couldn't a person just use that every month?" Dalton asked as he took a few strips of bacon from the plate.

"It would make you lethargic and unable to do anything, and pretty soon the Wolf's Bane and Silver would build to toxic levels in your body. Larger and larger doses would be needed as your body became accustomed to the mixture like the fixes of an addict."

"So, the cure would end up killing me?"

"Something like that." Julia put slices of crisp bacon between her pieces of toast. "I'm gonna take my bath when I finish this and then we can run out to Mom's and make certain everything is set there."

After eating, Julia added her ritual oils to the wooden chest holding the items necessary to perform her duties as High Priestess of the DuBois Coven during the ritual that night. Dalton carried it to the sporty blue car. They drove in silence to the DuBois mansion where they saw Antione De la Croix's black limousine parked in the circular drive.

"Looks like the Big Kahuna is here," Dalton said with a chuckle.

"Yah, Mom hosted him and Sandra Benet last night. The rest of their covens are at the hotel or farmed out to other DuBois members."

"Just exactly how many are there?"

"There are twelve in each Circle and their priestess or priest. We'll have four circles, so there will be over fifty people out there performing the ritual." Julia parked her car in front of the white garage doors of the converted carriage house.

"Where the hell did you find room for all those people to bed down?"

"Well, the Bourbons aren't coming out until today. They didn't want to stay out here in the swamp any longer than they had to." Julia huffed. "And they're all driving back to New Orleans after they get back into St. Elizabeth tonight."

"How long will this ritual thing take?"

"The ritual itself will only take about an hour, but ferrying everybody back out in the dark is going to take forever." Julia and Dalton walked through the picket gate onto the patio where several people sat in Adirondack chairs sipping hot coffee or tea. "Hey, Mom, it looks like you had a full house last night."

"That I did," Ruby said cheerfully. Antoine came with some of the Bourbon. It was tight, but we made do."

With surprise, Julia saw Laura Bourbon sitting in one of the deep-seated chairs, looking as though she was reluctantly sitting around a fire on a camping trip in the wilderness. She swatted at nonexistent mosquitoes and fanned her face with a silk fan.

Julia couldn't believe this woman had actually descended from the French royal family. She had heard stories about the family, accused of witchcraft by the Inquisition, and how they'd been exiled to the New World because they were members of the royal family and couldn't be executed. That had been long before the French Revolution when the Bourbon family in France were all hunted down and beheaded.

That family had made the first settlement and coven in the New World for witches. When the Puritans began their purge and hangings in the English Colonies, the Bourbon family let it be known that there was refuge and sanctuary in Canada for those who still practiced the old religions.

Julia looked now at this smug woman and shook her head. Was this really the legacy of such a great old French family?

"Do you have everything we need, sweetheart?" Ruby asked, shaking Julia back to the present and the task at hand.

"Yes, Dalton got the ATVs to the site and has arranged for large airboats to take us upriver with pilots to make more than one trip to ferry us back and forth. Mary has all her things taken care of, though she's not taking part in the ritual. The binding potion is ready and oils have been extracted from all the things we collected to anoint the men.

"Why aren't *all* of your coven members taking part when this is *your* problem?" Laura asked in a snide tone.

"Mary has health problems that make her attendance impossible," Ruby DuBois said from her chair. "I'll be taking her place in the Circle."

"Mom," Julia said in surprise, "do you think that's a good idea? You've only been out of the hospital a little over a week and the doctor said to take it easy."

"I'll be perfectly fine, Priestess," Ruby spoke formally to her daughter. "I owe this to your father and your brother."

"And I owe it to both *my* parents," said a small stern voice from behind them, "and my grandpa."

Julia turned to see Melanie standing with her hands resolutely on her narrow, young hips. She completely understood her niece's need to take part in the ceremony. "You are more than welcome, future priestess of the DuBois. You will stand by my side in the Circle." Julia spoke formally as well. "The DuBois and their friends will perform this ceremony in the memory of those we have lost, and because we are righting a grievous wrong done to innocent men by another Coven. Harm has been done and we are guided by the Reade to undo that harm. We do as we will, but we harm no other." Julia directed the last sentence toward Melanie.

Several, including Antione De la Croix, stood and bowed to Julia. "We are happy to assist you, Priestess of the DuBois. We lend our strength. So mote it be."

'So mote it be' was repeated throughout the group. Julia

125

smiled at the phrase, which was the Wiccan equivalent of Captain Pickard's 'Make it so' on Star Trek.

Julia took Dalton's sturdy hand. "Shall we go?"

"Yes, ma'am," he replied respectfully.

"Tables are there to set up for the men to lie on during the ritual, as well as the makings of a bonfire. I think we have everything. Dalton and I are going down to the dock now and taking a boat up to the site to get things started. Does anyone want to join us?"

"I'm going," Melanie volunteered.

Julia looked to her mother for guidance, but the older woman only shrugged her shoulders and smiled. Julia put her arm around Melanie's shoulder. "Ok, kiddo, let's go, but it's a long ride in the boat and it's really out in the wilderness. You might not get phone reception out there."

"Really?" Melanie asked, holding her phone in her hands.

"I only got one bar when I was out there. I can't guarantee anything."

"Oh well," Melanie slid her phone into the back pocket of her jeans. "That's OK, I guess. I want to help."

They drove to the dock on the Vermillion River and stowed away the bags of Big Macs and fries they'd picked up for lunch with the men. It would all be cold by the time they got there with it, but Julia didn't think the deprived men would complain.

"Lenny's not working here anymore," Dalton said before starting the engine. "They said he just stopped coming to work and nobody can get him on his phone."

"I wonder where De la Croix has them all stashed. He has a huge house in the Garden District, but I don't know if he has dungeons in the basement." Julia chuckled before taking a sip of her root beer.

"I hope they're all in dungeons and Mr. De la Croix throws away the key," Melanie shouted over the roar of the big fan behind her. "I just wish they'd got that Althea woman. She was a priestess and should have known better than to have broken the

Reade. Grandpa always said that was our most important Council Law and the oldest."

It did Julia good to hear the girl say that. She hoped Melanie would embrace and follow them. Julia didn't want Melanie to think she should use witchcraft to exact revenge. "Your grandpa was right, and it's important that you remember it and what can happen when a witch breaks that law."

"People die." The wind blew the girls blonde hair back from her little face as Julia watched her pop a fry into her mouth.

They rode in silence and Julia enjoyed the lush scenery around her. On one side of the river grew thick vegetation and tall cypress trees with their massive trunks. Sphagnum moss hung from branches and danced in the wind blowing through the trees. Vines draped between smaller trees and bushes. Julia caught the scents of honeysuckle and Jasmine over the dank fishy smell of the river and places where water stood around the big trees. Julia saw the diaphanous webs of the huge black and yellow spiders that made the insect-rich swamp their home. She shivered just thinking about them.

On the other side of the river stood fields of sugarcane. Farmhands would soon be setting fires in those fields to burn off the undergrowth, so the cane could be harvested. For now, however, the cane stood tall and green in the fields. Cranes and herons rested upon their spindly legs, poking long beaks into the shallows to pluck up small fish, frogs, and crayfish for their lunches.

Julia loved the swamp and its abundance of life. Tonight, she and her friends would draw their power from that life to counter the curses set upon the eight men. She prayed to the Goddess they would be successful.

The glen didn't sit more than twelve miles downriver from the small town of Covington. Julia wondered how the men had not ventured toward it in their transformed states to hunt the human prey craved by the *loup-garou*. One of the major reasons the curse had been created eons ago by a witch jilted by her lover was to cause a man, when transformed, to want human meat and human blood. The cursed man would then be wracked with guilt over his kills for the whole month between changes when he knew he'd kill again. Norm and the others must have had powerful resolve not to move closer to humans.

Dalton slowed the boat as they neared Old Man Tree, and he pointed it out to Melanie. "You see that big dead tree there, Mel?" He pointed to the towering skeleton of the massive tree. "That tree there was only a sprout when Moses parted the Red Sea."

Melanie looked to her aunt. "What's he talking about?"

"Moses is a man in the Christian Bible who helped to save his enslaved people from a Pharaoh in Egypt. He was leading them to Israel and had to part the sea so they could walk across."

"Oh yeah, I saw that in a movie. Did it really happen?" Melanie asked, wide-eyed. "That would be some real powerful magic."

"It was the power of God that did it," Dalton said.

"It's what the Christian faith believes." Julia shrugged her shoulders. "Perhaps Moses was a powerful wizard and he could draw his power from all of those following him." Julia looked at Dalton who rolled his eyes.

"So, you mean that tree was there when the Pharaohs ruled Egypt?" Melanie asked skeptically. "That was, like, three thousand years ago. I don't think cypress trees live *that* long."

"Well, that one is dead and has been dead since I was your age." Dalton gave in to the educated nine year-old. "It was just something my grandpa used to say."

Melanie touched Dalton's hand. "Grandpas are worth listening to;" she muttered softly. "They know more than *we* probably ever will."

Dalton finished his Coke, looked at Julia, and smiled. "Out of the mouths of babes." He restarted the engine and they moved on toward the shallows.

## 18

D alton ran the airboat upon the bank and shut off the engine. Lined up before them in the tall grass were a dozen ATVs and leaning against one of them were four folded massage tables.

"I suppose we'd better get to it," Dalton said, climbing down from the boat. "It's gonna take a few trips to get all this stuff up there." He motioned toward the tables and the cardboard boxes full of candles and incense. "It looks like the guys have already carried the wood for the bonfire up there." Dalton took Julia's ritual chest from the back of the boat and handed her the McDonalds bags. He carried a cooler filled with ice, beer, and sodas. He strapped it to the back of one of the all-terrain vehicles. "Can you drive one of these, Jules? I don't think the three of us will fit on one with all of this stuff."

*"I can drive one,"* Melanie volunteered with a smile. *"Grandpa taught me."* It took Dalton a minute to realize the girl's voice was in his head and not his ears.

*"If it's OK with your aunt."* Dalton replied with his thoughts.

Julia shrugged. *"It's OK with me. Dad taught me, too."* Julia went to a vehicle and climbed on. She turned the key in the ignition. Glancing at the bags of food at her feet, Julia hoped they would make the rough ride without vibrating off. She waited for Dalton to strap the ritual chest onto the back of Melanie's ATV and the cooler onto his.

*"Here we go,"* Dalton projected and threw his vehicle into gear.

All three of them rode through the tall grass and razor-sharp saw palmetto until they came upon the group of men sitting and standing under the shade of a leafy oak. Julia was glad to see they'd made use of the toiletries she'd sent and had shaved, washed, and cut their hair. All the men wore clean shorts and t-shirts.

"Hi, fellas," Julia said and picked up the white bags of food. "We brought lunch, but I'm afraid it's probably cold."

Larry Peters stepped forward and took the bags with a broad smile on his clean-shaven face. "That's more than OK." He passed the bags to some of the other men who grabbed them hungrily.

"I brought the beer," Dalton said, smiling, "and it's definitely cold." He opened the cooler and began passing around cans of Bud. He handed Melanie a Coke which she accepted with a frown.

*"Grandpa let me drink beer."*

*"Don't get carried away, Mel."* Julia chided. *"You're only nine. You'll have to wait a few more years for beer."*

Julia picked up her bag of food and walked into the shade with the others. She handed Dalton a Big Mac and a cardboard carton of fries. Melanie wrinkled her nose at the cold offering and sat cross-legged in the thin grass under the leafy tree. She stared warily at the seven gaunt men around her stuffing their mouths with the burgers and fries.

*"How long have they been here like this? They're eating like they haven't seen food in like forever."*

*"Less than a year,"* Julia replied, biting into her sandwich and enjoying the taste of the tangy sauce on her tongue, though the meat was cold. *"But too long for any man."*

"Where do you guys sleep?" Melanie asked with a deep furrow on her brow.

"We sleep under the trees and up under the bushes." A blonde man whose handsome face was marred by a jagged scar answered.

"What's your name?" Melanie asked. Julia was glad to see her niece's easy manner with the strange men around her.

"I'm Howie," he stammered. "Howie Denehey. I lived in Abbeville until I got tangled up with Althea Rubidoux."

"How long have you been out here?" Melanie appeared to be full of questions.

"Me and my girl, Tanya, came here six moons ago." He looked away, but took a drink of his beer.

"I didn't know there are women here too," Melanie said, wide-eyed.

"She's not here anymore." Howie nodded toward a balding man sitting a little apart. "Tom's girlfriend Kelly got turned, too. Both girls are dead now." He rubbed at the scar on his jaw. "During the turn things get pretty rough. We're all just a bunch of animals. We fight with one another over everything. We fought over the women the most. They were animals too and fought back."

Howie emptied the beer in one long swallow, watching Tom. "I guess I killed Kelly. During the change we don't know what we're doing really. It's all simply animal instinct. I wanted to ..." He glanced from Melanie to Julia and Dalton. "Well, I guess I wanted to mate and she didn't. We fought and Kelly died from her injuries." He touched the scar on his face again and tears came to his eyes. Howie stood abruptly and fled from the shade.

Tom gave a long sigh and put his burger atop his carton of fries. "I'll go talk to him ... again." The smaller man followed Howie into the field and put a hand on his heaving shoulders.

"Who killed Howie's girlfriend?" Melanie asked, looking around the circle of men. "What happened to *her*?"

"Tanya died after her first change." Larry said softly. "Some of the guys who'd been here for a long time hadn't had a female in a while. I guess it got pretty rough."

*"Does he mean they sexed her to death?"* Melanie projected in a disgusted tone.

*"I think that's what he meant, sweetheart, but don't be overly harsh on them. The change lowers them to their basest animal instincts: eat, fight, and mate. They had no choice in the matter."*

"She's right, Mel." Dalton added. *"It's horrible. All you think about is the chase and you won't let anything get in your way."*

"What are all your names?" Melanie changed the subject and the men, looking confused by their long silence gave their names. Along with Larry Peters, Howie Denehey, and Tom Galloway were Dan Blanc, Randy Lemieux, Marv Thibodaux, and Bill Dumont. Julia remembered most of their names from the rumor mill or missing person fliers. All had family or friends who'd been looking for them. Marv Thibodaux was the missing Thibodaux cousin, suspected of causing the crash that killed the family. Julia wanted to get his side of the story and find out what Althea and her coven had really done and why.

They needed the men's names for the ritual along with a bit of their hair or nails and Julia was glad Melanie had asked. The leader of each Circle would collect those bits of bodily material from the men they would be working with. Julia took in the faces around her. All the men looked pitiful, but hopeful.

Over the next few hours they retrieved and set up the four massage tables in the center of the glen. Melanie and Dalton had run their ATVs in a large circle to flatten the grass and waist-high brambles. While the afflicted men made a pile of wood in the location specified by Julia for the bonfire, she organized the ritual items she'd need for the ceremony. The petit High Priestess of the DuBois ran the words of the ritual through her head once more and rechecked it in her ancient Grimoire, making certain she had it set to memory properly.

A chill took Julia as she thought of what could happen if the bindings didn't work and these men made the change with the rising of the full moon. She watched Melanie, laughing on the ATV, and wondered again if it had been wise, after all, to include the child. Julia understood Melanie's desire to exact some form of revenge for her parents' and beloved grandfather's deaths, but perhaps this was not the way. The danger of these men changing into vicious beasts might be too great. She, her mother, her niece, and her friends were taking their lives into their hands doing this ritual. In essence, the whole DuBois line and coven could be wiped out tonight, along with those of three others. It was a huge risk to take, but looking at the poor men around her, Julia knew it would be worth it.

"Do you think we need more wood, Miss DuBois?" Larry Peters asked, shaking Julia from her thoughts.

"No, that looks good. Is there plenty of small stuff to get it going?"

"I think so. Are we going to set it before sunset?"

"Yes, we'll get it going before five," Julia said. "My mom will be here by then to give all y'all the binding potion to prevent the change. It will make you sleepy, so we'll put you on the tables and bind your hands and feet. I doubt it would hold you if you actually changed, but the ritual demands it. The ties have been soaking in the solution for a few days now and have been blessed."

"Do you think this mumbo-jumbo will really work?"

"The mumbo-jumbo Althea used to make you this way worked, didn't it." Julia closed her Grimoire with a loud slam and sighed. "I'm sorry, Larry. I didn't mean to be short with you." She reached up and took the man's hand. "I suppose I'm just a little nervous."

"Yeah, so are we." Larry sat next to her on the moldering leaves under the big oak. "We want it to work, of course, but we're all worried about what we'll be going back to. My wife is gone now and my job, I'd imagine." He ran a hand through his roughly trimmed brown hair. "We have no believable explanations for our absences. I suppose I could say I ran away because of the pressures of my job combined with my wife's illness, but that's not going to earn me any points with anyone." Larry pulled a cold beer from the cooler and offered one to Julia, who declined.

"You'd better make that your last one. Mixing alcohol with the potion might not be a good idea."

"Oh, sure. I didn't think about that." He yelled to his fellows. "Last call for alcohol, guys. The lady says the beer might not go good with the magic."

One-by-one the men came and collected one last beer, including Dalton who bent and gave Julia a quick kiss. "You're the best, Jules, and Mel is a real trooper. That kid really knows her witchy stuff. She's been filling me in on life in a magical family." Dalton grinned and continued using his telepathy. *"We've been practicing with telepathy, too. She thinks she and her brother have been pulling the wool over grandma's eyes."*

*"You didn't tell her, did you? Mom wants to spring it on them in her own time."*

*"No, I let her go on thinking she and Benny are doing something cool."*

*"Thanks, babe. How is she doing with tonight?"*

*"She's excited."* Dalton said. *"I don't think she's given any thought to what might happen if things don't go as planned."*

*"I guess that's good."* Julia sighed. *"I don't want her to fret about it. She has enough on her plate right now. You're very talented with the telepathy, Dalton. Keep practicing with Mel to keep her mind off things, please."*

*"Hell, it's keeping* my *mind off things."* Dalton walked back carrying a Coke to where Melanie sat on her ATV.

Julia watched him hand her the cold can and saw her niece's face brighten with a smile. This man is the complete package. She couldn't believe her good luck in finding him. She watched him laughing with Melanie and Julia's worries about the night began to melt away.

At around three-thirty, they heard the whine of engines and

saw three ATVs rolling up from the river. Julia recognized Tom's long white hair flying in the breeze, Hal's bulky body, and to her surprise, Ruby DuBois. The vehicles parked and Melanie ran into her grandmother's arms.

"I haven't seen you on one of those in ages, Mom," Julia said with a grin on her face.

"Your dad and I used to ride all the time." Ruby attempted to get off the vehicle, wincing in pain as her hip and knees protested the abuse.

Dalton rushed to her side and helped Ruby from the ATV. "You should have ridden on the back, Mrs. DuBois. It would have been easier on you."

"Son, this body may be old, but it certainly isn't ready to give up." She turned to Julia. "I'm going to look into hip surgery after all of this, though."

"It's about time," Julia said. "Dad was after you to do that years ago."

"I know," Ruby sighed out, and took a seat upon the cooler in the shade of the big oak. "I just didn't want to think about hospital food, surgery, and months of physical therapy afterward, but now I need both knees and the damned hip replaced." She smiled down at Melanie who now sat on the ground by the cooler. "Grandma will be a bionic woman when the doctors are finished with me." Julia saw the confusion on her niece's face at the reference to the old television program.

The men began to congregate around the newcomers. Julia introduced them. Some gave Ruby the short version of their stories. When Larry Peters shook Ruby's hand, Julia heard her mother.

"I knew your sweet wife, son. I wish we could have done more for her."

"Excuse me?" Larry asked with his brow furrowed in confusion.

"My daughter asked the Goddess for healing blessings, but we didn't have everything we needed to do a full healing ceremony. Not long after our ritual, though, Annie slipped into a coma, and peace."

"I thank you for that, ma'am. Did you know my wife?"

"Only in passing. Her mother was a friend from my school days, but didn't know about any of this." Ruby nodded toward the coven's ritual chest sitting on the moldering ground. "If she had, perhaps I could have approached her about it."

"I understand, ma'am." Larry shook his head sadly. "I wouldn't have believed any of this could actually have happened a year ago, but here we are. I remember my granny telling us stories about witches out on the island and how they could curse folks, but you know how it goes."

"Indeed, I do. We have kept our secrets out here because of just that reason."

Tom glanced at Ruby and then Julia. "Are y'all gonna do anything to us so we won't remember any of this and keep your secrets?"

"I don't think that will be necessary, son. As our Dalton here pointed out the other day, who would believe it? We've been shielded by the plethora of supernatural television shows and movies over the years. Nobody believes in it anymore. If any of you began telling stories about witches, curses, and *loup-garou*, you'd end up in the State Hospital."

"But people believe in ghosts and haunted houses because of those ghost-hunter shows," Tom argued.

"Do they really?" Ruby asked and stood up to probe the ice in the cooler for a Coke. "I believe most people think it's a bunch of hooey. If any of those fools actually encountered a spirit they'd shit their pants. That, I'd like to see." Ruby laughed and returned the lid to the insulated plastic box before sitting.

"Are there really ghosts?" Howie asked.

"Of course there are, young man. After this has happened to you, how can you doubt it? Have you not sensed the spirit that's attached to you?"

"It's his girlfriend, Tonya," Melanie said, and everyone stared at the girl. "She's sitting right by him."

"You see spirits?" Ruby asked her granddaughter in awe. "That's a true gift. Have you sensed your parents or your grandfather?"

"Grandpa hangs out by the fire pit in his chair. He didn't like that silly Laura woman sitting in his chair. He worries about you," Melanie said sadly to her grandmother. "I haven't seen Mom or Dad, but they may be at our house and not yours. They also might be stuck out there where they died. Grandpa says he can't leave the house or the patio. That's where he died, right?"

"That would make sense." Ruby tousled her granddaughter's hair. "After this is over we'll drive out to the old orchard and see if they're there. We'll take Benny, too, so they can see the both of you."

"That would be awesome, Grandma." Melanie wrapped her arms around Ruby's neck, her eyes full of tears, but she had a broad smile on her delicate face.

9

B efore dusk, Tom and Hal lit the bonfire while Julia made
certain the men drank the binding potion and were tied
upon the massage tables.

"Damn," Randy Lemieux shook his shaggy black head and
spat as he took the first hesitant sip of the binding potion. "This
shit burns like hell. You sure it's not poison?"

"It would be poison to anyone else," Julia said calmly, "but not to
all y'all. It's just going to make you sleepy and keep you from going
into the change during the ceremony." She looked around at the
others who held their cups tentatively. "Go on now, drink it down."
When they continued to hesitate, she prodded. "Oh come on. Don't
be a bunch of babies. Just pretend it's a shot of Jack and throw it
back." Julia slapped Dalton on the shoulder, surprised he still sat
staring at his cup. "Come on, babe, show the boys how it's done."

Julia heard gagging and looked over to see Larry Peters and
Tom sipping the potions. "Oh my god," Tom gasped, "this burns
like biting into a tabasco pepper right off the plant. I don't think I
can swallow it all."

"Sure you can," Dalton said and drained his Styrofoam cup.
"Ahhh," he said red-faced and sweating after swallowing the

138

mixture. "I wouldn't recommend it for our next party, but it's done." He dropped the crumpled cup into a waiting trash bag. "Come on, y'all, drink up. The ladies spent hours slaving over a boiling cauldron chanting double bubble, toil and trouble over this shit. You don't want to piss 'em off or you're likely to end up on the receiving end of the frog spell and there ain't no princesses here in Louisiana to break that one."

Julia gave him a smile and a wink as the others gagged down the odious mixture as best they could. "You're cruel, Dalton, but I love you and, technically, I think Laura Bourbon is probably a princess."

He rolled his eyes, bent over, and kissed Julia, the sting of the potion still burning his lips. "I love you too, Jules, and I'm sure these guys will too when this night is over."

Julia rolled her eyes and looked at the green-faced men. "I hope you're right, babe. I still have to tell three of them they have to drink an extra half cup because they've been cursed longer than the rest. I get the feeling they aren't going to be happy about it."

"You're probably right about that. This stuff is bitter as hell and burns like fire going down. It's all I can do to keep from bringin' it back up."

"Randy," Julia said, pouring more mixture into cups, "I need you, Larry, and Dan to drink a little more." She heard them groan in protest. "It's only a half a cup, but Mary said you have to have the additional doses because you've made more changes and will be harder to bind."

"Please, fellas," Dalton pleaded, "it's gonna be sunset soon and we don't want to take any chances, especially with the kid here." He nodded toward the bright-eyed Melanie, who'd captured all their hearts in her short time around them, offering a quick smile and a warm heart to all of the men. The men took the cups, closed their eyes and downed the liquid in one long swallow.

Melanie and Ruby then attended to the cords to bind the hands and feet of all the men upon the tables.

"Aren't they going to be uncomfortable, Grandma?" Melanie asked with sympathy for the restrained men.

"It has to be done this way, sweetheart." Ruby said as she secured the final cord around a dozing Dalton's ankles. All the men were naked, but Julia didn't think Melanie even noticed. Considering the girl was only nine years old, she radiated an air of maturity well beyond her age. Julia couldn't be more proud.

All the ATVs except two had been returned to the river and other coven members had begun to arrive in groups of four to six. Candles were lit and Circles drawn by the priest and priestesses. They held their collective breaths as the bright moon rose in the sky above the glittering waters of the bayou. Julia watched the men struggle some in their bonds, but none, to her great relief, made the change. She made the sign of the pentagram over her breast and whispered a prayer of thanks to the Goddess. She saw others in the glen doing the same.

As the moon reached the point in the sky prescribed by the additional notation in her Grimoire, Julia raised her arms and began the ritual chant to reverse the *loup-garou* curse. She watched the others clad in their robes do the same. Soon the chanting of the four covens filled the unnaturally silent glen. No crickets or tree frogs chirped, no owls hooted from the limbs of the tall oaks, and no bats swooped in to feast upon insects drawn by the flickering light of the bonfire and candles. The yipping of coyotes and roars of alligators in the area had gone silent as the witches drew power from the creatures of the verdant swamplands around them.

Julia inhaled the cleansing scent of the frankincense and myrrh she'd oiled her body with before beginning the ritual. The men had all been anointed with the preparation mixed by Mary for the ceremony and the scent of honeysuckle wafted at Julia on the heavy, damp air. She raised her black-handled Athame into the night sky and invoked the powers of the east, west, north, south and the universe, drawing the sign of the pentagram in the air above her head. She called down the Goddess and begged her to intercede on the behalf of these wretched souls and lift the curse that had been cast upon them.

The power being drawn into the respective circles was palpable, and raised the hair upon Julia's arms. Her spine tingled with the electricity in the air. Melanie stood beside her aunt with her skinny arms raised, reading along from the book of spells. Julia could feel the child pulling power into her along with the adults throughout the glen, and it filled her with pride. Melanie would, indeed, be a fine High Priestess of the DuBois one day.

As the final words of the chant to reverse the *loup-garou* curse passed Julia's lips, Dalton bolted upright on the table before her and his eyes flew open. The steely blue irises reflected the flickering firelight around the glen.

"What have you done, bitch," Dalton's voice snarled. Julia knew, however, the person glaring at her through Dalton's handsome eyes was not Dalton, but Althea Rubidoux.

"I've countered your evil, Althea."

"You couldn't have. That curse was binding. Your tiny coven couldn't possibly have channeled enough power to counter my curse upon Dalton La Pierre."

"Not just Dalton's curse, Althea. We've countered the curses you cast upon the others here as well."

"And she wasn't alone, Miss Rubidoux," boomed the voice of Antoine De la Croix from behind Julia. "But you are no longer Rubidoux. That name has been stripped from you and stricken from the list of covens. You go nameless now."

"You may have taken my name, Antoine, but you cannot take my power." Althea spoke boldly through Dalton's mouth.

"When you are found, girl, I'll have your head." Antoine spat. "You murdered your own priestess. That is an offence punishable by death."

"If I'm found, you mean. Your lackeys haven't been very successful yet, Antoine," Althea sneered and laughed.

From the darkness, Melanie rushed forward. The slip of a girl flitted past them into the Circle, reached her arm up, and slapped her palm to Dalton's sweaty forehead. Julia watched as her niece's blue eyes rolled back into her head and she stood perfectly still, drawing power from the quiet world around her. Others began to filter over from the other Circles. They could all feel the little witch drawing power and some deliberately channeled to Melanie, adding their strength to hers.

Ruby stepped to Julia's side. "What's going on, Julia? What is Melanie doing?"

"Althea's taken Dalton again." Julia took her mother's hand. "I'm not sure what Mel is doing."

"It's not safe, Julia," Ruby begged. "Melanie is a telepath. That evil bitch could do something to her if she knows how to back-channel her power." Ruby began to move toward her granddaughter in the candlelit circle.

"No, Mom, let this play out for a while." Julia stopped her mother with a restraining hand upon her shoulder. "Mel has plenty of protection here and power behind her."

"Very well, Priestess." Ruby bowed her head and stepped back. "I defer to you in this matter. It is your place to make this decision."

"She's in her room at her house on the island," Melanie called to them. "She's been there all along hiding like a coward."

Julia heard Antoine De la Croix making a phone call to relay the information.

Dalton's head shook, trying to throw off Melanie's hand. "Who's doing this?" Althea screeched. "Why can't I move?"

"Hold her there, child," Antoine said. "My people are on their way to the island from the docks now."

"What? No!" Althea screamed and thrashed as she heard Antoine's words through Dalton's ears.

Melanie pushed Dalton's writhing body back down upon the massage table and held him there. "Be quiet, bitch." Melanie muttered, pushing his head violently onto the small pillow on the narrow table. Dalton's body suddenly went slack.

As the sun peeked over the horizon, Julia watched men being helped from the massage tables. Melanie released her hold on Dalton and slumped to the ground beside the stainless steel legs of the table. Ruby and Julia rushed to the little girl's side.

"Are you all right, baby?" Ruby cooed as she took her granddaughter into her arms.

"The men came for her," Melanie said weakly from the safety of Ruby's grasp, before slipping into an exhausted sleep.

Antoine De la Croix bent and took the child from her grandmother. "This is one strong little witch," he said to Ruby. "The DuBois should be proud. Their future is secured in this one."

Julia turned to the big man. "I'm not quite in a rocking chair yet."

"Of course not, Priestess. You have much to teach this one." He hefted Melanie for her head to rest upon his broad shoulder. "She is in good hands with you and your mother to guide her, as will your daughter to come." He winked at Julia and patted her belly with his free hand. "That one," Antione nodded his bald head toward Dalton, who was sitting up now, "may wish he could have stayed out here in the bayou when he realizes he will have four strong DuBois witches to contend with very soon." He laughed in a deep baritone as he carried Melanie to one of the ATVs, followed closely by Ruby DuBois and several of the yawning coven members.

"What was the Big Kahuna going on about?" Dalton asked as he stood and stretched.

Julia clasped her hands around her midsection and smiled to herself. "I'm not sure. How are you feeling, babe?" She went to his side and put a freckled arm around his waist.

"My head's a little fuzzy, but I'm alright." Dalton kissed her. "Did it work? Are we cured?"

"I think so," Julia told him, "We took the bindings from all your hands and ankles an hour before moonset and none of you went into the change." She looked up at him and smiled. "I'd say it was successful. You should probably all come back out here next moon to be certain, but I think it's done. Althea certainly was pissed about it."

"What?" Dalton asked, wide-eyed. "What happened?"

Julia spent the next half hour explaining the occurrences of the early morning and Melanie's brave intervention.

"De la Croix's people have Althea? You're certain?"

"He confirmed it with one of his men on the phone after Melanie said they had her. She's on her way back to New Orleans in lead shackles and chains."

"What will they do with her?" Larry Peters asked as he helped to fold the nearest massage table for transport back to the boats.

"I'm not sure," Julia admitted. "There will be a trial before the heads of all the covens. All y'all will have to come testify."

"You mean like a real trial in court?" Tom asked. "Has she been arrested by the law?"

"She and her people have been taken into custody by our law officials and will be tried in a court of our High Council."

"What kind of justice will that serve?" Howie asked sullenly. "How will she pay for the lives of Tonya, Kelly, and the others who took their lives because there was no hope for them? How will she and her people pay for them and for all the suffering we endured out here all these months, and have yet to endure, trying to put our lives back together?"

"We can talk about it later, buddy," Dalton said, slapping a hand on Howie's shoulder. "Suffice it to say, these witches mete out justice appropriate to the crime." He looked down at Julia and smiled. "I don't know 'bout all y'all but I sure could go for some pancakes and sausage at La Petit Paris with a big pot of hot coffee."

They finished folding and stacking the tables onto ATVs, used the water in the cooler to douse the final embers in the bonfire, and strapped everything down to make their way back to the waiting airboats. Dalton would have the vehicles collected in a few days and returned to their owners. As they drove the bumpy track back to the banks of the Vermillion River, Julia breathed in the fresh, cool breeze blowing across the bayou and whispered a thank you to all the creatures of the swamp that aided in their ritual the night before.

None took more from any creature than they could afford to give, but Julia knew the swamp would be quiet and peaceful for a day or two as all rebuilt their strength. Dalton might be longing for pancakes and sausage, but Julia longed for the comfort of her mattress and pillows. As the airboat came into view, the thought of the hour-long ride back down the river only deepened her fatigue.

## 20

Their official invitation to The Witches' Ball included an additional summons to testify at the trial of Althea and the defunct Rubidoux Coven.

The moon following the ritual did not see any of the men make the change. The ritual for the counter-curse had worked flawlessly. Julia had kept tabs on the men and most had settled back in, if uneasily, with family and friends. Howie and Tom had become roommates in Tom's mother's home. Larry Peters returned to a job at the bank, but not his former position as head loan officer. He'd been reluctantly given a position in the collections department. His family took him back with open arms, but those of his late wife's shunned him and circulated rumors that he'd been away with a mistress while his wife had suffered and died in his absence. Julia felt for him, but there was nothing she or her coven could do, but ignore the rumors and do nothing to spread them further.

As the celebration of Samhain approached, Julia and Dalton found they had something more to celebrate.

Dalton walked into the bathroom one morning to find Julia sitting quietly upon the toilet staring at a plastic wand. "What's that, Jules?" He asked as he reached in to turn on the shower.

"Look for yourself," Julia said and handed him the purple plastic stick with a circular space marked with a small black plus sign.

"What's this?" He stared at it for a moment before she handed him the cardboard packaging the stick had come from. "This is a pregnancy test?" He stood looking from the box to the stick and back to her. "You're pregnant? Oh my god." Dalton stared down at her, dropped the box and the wand into the waste can, and lifted Julia to her feet. "Oh my god. You're pregnant." He twirled her around in the center of the narrow bathroom with a broad smile on his face. "You mean we're gonna have a baby?"

"Well, one of us is." Julia laughed. "I'll be doing the having while you stand by waiting for her to pop out."

"Her? You know it's going to be a girl already?" Julia thought he sounded disappointed.

"A little bird named Antoine gave me a hint when we were out in the bayou."

"Oh well, I suppose that cinches it, then. If the Big Kahuna says it's a girl, I guess it's a girl."

"Will you be that disappointed if it is?" Julia asked him with her lower lip stuck out in a pout.

"Of course not, Jules." He said, and kissed her soundly on the mouth. "When is our little witch going to get here?"

Julia did some quick math in her head. "June or July. I'll call for an appointment with a midwife today."

"A midwife and not a doctor?"

Julia raised an eyebrow. "Really, Dalton?"

He threw his arms up into the air. "OK, OK. I give. A midwife it is. Will you at least go to a hospital or will you have our kid out on a blanket in the backyard?"

"Probably in a tub of warm water on Mom's patio."

"Are you serious?" He looked at her in dismay.

"That's where both Melanie and Benny were born."

"Oh my god, Jules. Seriously?" Dalton sat down on the toilet and ran a hand through his sandy-blonde curls.

"I don't know what the big deal is, Dalton. Women have babies standing up in mud huts in Africa. I'll be at my mom's with a certified midwife and if she thinks it's warranted I *will* go to the hospital."

"Damned straight you will. No kid of mine is going to be born in a mud hut."

"No, in a pool of warm water so she won't be too shocked. After floating around for nine months in warm water, it's best if she's born into it. You can look it up on the internet if you want to." Julia assured him, patting the top of his head. "I'm gonna call my mom now with the news."

"You mean *she* didn't know already?" Dalton called after her, laughing.

"No, but Mel may have. They could be talking already," Julia said with a mischievous smile.

"Oh, great. You're all going to be ganging up on me, aren't you? She's not even born yet and you'll have her conspiring against me."


The moon shone bright and full on Samhain night in the Garden District of New Orleans. At a sprawling prestigious mansion, men and women wearing formal attire arrived in luxury auto-mobiles and were escorted into the inner sanctum of the brightly lit building. Many spoke in hushed tones, but none laughed or joked on this solemn occasion.

As the final few arrived and took their seats, the wide double doors of the room were closed and locked. Huge, muscle-bound men in black suits and ties stood watch to make certain no unwelcome guests tried to enter and that none tried to leave once the proceedings had begun.

Julia in an emerald green, velvet gown sat beside Dalton,

who wore a tux. He tugged at the tight collar and Julia slapped at his hand.

"Sit still, Dalton," she fussed, "this is an important event."

"Yes, dear," Ruby DuBois, wearing black velvet added, "we must appear to be the picture of backwater gentry."

"Oh, Mother," Julia scolded, "will you please be serious. This is a very important night."

Sitting between her grandmother and Dalton, Melanie sat wearing a bright blue, floor-length dress. She giggled at Dalton's discomfort in the stuffy room.

"I know it's important, daughter. If De la Croix sentences the bitch to the stake, I brought the match to light the fucking fire."

Dalton gave Julia's mother a high-five and choked back a laugh in his throat.

"I don't know what I'm going to do with the two of you, but if you don't start acting appropriately, I'm sending you both to the back of the room," Julia said sternly, but suppressed a smile.

"Oyez, Oyez," a loud voice boomed. "Attend ye now to this High Court of the De la Croix Council on this most holy of nights." A wooden staff struck upon the floor, quieting the people in the crowded room.

Julia sat straighter in her seat as Antoine De la Croix stepped upon the dais wearing a black robe trimmed in gold at the wide cuffs and collar. His bald black head gleamed in the light of flickering torches set into the walls of the huge room.

"I bid you good evening, fellow coven leaders and friends." Antoine spoke in his deep baritone. "We are here tonight to hear testimony as to the crimes of murder, of breaking the High Council Laws of The Reade, and of the use of the foul *Loup-garou* curse brought forth against Althea once of the Rubidoux, and that now defunct coven. Bring forth the accused."

The doors opened at the back of the room, and a line of men and women dressed in thin white robes and shackled together with heavy chains filed in. At their head, bowed and broken with a shaved head, limped Althea. Her once beautiful face now bore bruises and her full lips were cracked and bleeding.

"Looks like they worked her over good," Dalton whispered into Julia's ear. "Why the heavy chains and shackles? It's not like they're going to run any place."

"They're shackled and chained in lead," Julia replied. "It absorbs their power and keeps them from drawing any in. Lead shields magic."

"You mean like around a nuclear reactor?" Dalton asked in an awed tone.

"Yes. Power is power and lead has the same effect."

"Wow, radiation, Superman, and witches' magic too. Pretty good shit to have around. I'll keep that in mind."

Julia patted Dalton's hand resting on her lap. "We'll talk about it later, but there was a good reason for lead paint and leaded glass."

"We now ask our first witness to attend us. Mr. Dalton La Pierre, please come forward," the Herald called.

Dalton stood up and inched past the people seated in the row of chairs. He straightened his suit coat and walked to the front of the big room. Althea glared at him as he walked forward and Dalton couldn't help feeling apprehension as he stepped upon the dais to sit in the heavy chair next to the place where Althea and her associates stood. He saw Jerry amongst them and felt a pang of sympathy for the trembling man whose glasses were missing from his bruised and pock-marked face. Lenny from the marina stood next to Jerry with his head bowed.

"Mr. La Pierre," Antoine De la Croix began. "Can you explain to us what befell you at the hands of Althea of the Rubidoux Coven?"

"Yes, sir," Dalton replied respectfully. "I had been dating Althea ... Miss Rubidoux for about eight months, but decided it wasn't working out and began seeing Miss Julia DuBois." Dalton looked into the crowd to see Julia smiling at him. It bolstered his confidence and he continued. "After I broke up with her at a restaurant in town, she followed me to Julia's and made a scene. She threatened both Julia and me."

"And then what happened?" De la Croix asked.

"A couple of days later I woke up in a field naked and bloody. Althea was there and she told me I was now a *loup-garou*."

"And you knew what that was?" De la Croix inquired.

"Everybody in the bayou knows what it is. It's the old French word for werewolf. My grandpa told us all about them when we were kids."

"And was anybody else in attendance that morning?"

Dalton looked sadly at Jerry. "Yes, an acquaintance from high school, Jerry Malone."

"Is that man here today?"

"Yes, sir, he is, but I'd like to say something in his defense, if I may."

De la Croix looked irritated with Dalton. "I suppose. This is *your* testimony."

"If it weren't for Jerry, I wouldn't have known to go to Julia about the counter-curse. He took pity on me and steered me in that direction. He's not a bad guy. He was forced into it by Althea because she's family. I don't think he really wanted to hurt me or any of the others."

"Thank you Mr. La Pierre, but that will be for the Council to determine. Did you have any other interaction with Miss Rubidoux after you found you'd been cursed?"

"You mean like when she took over my body using her psychic connection with me?"

"Yes, Mr. La Pierre," De la Croix said, rolling his eyes. "Like that. How many times did she use her powers to psychically invade you?"

Dalton heard twittering laughter run through the crowded room and the Herald pounded his staff on the floor to quiet them so Dalton could answer.

"Three that I'm aware of, but I was having nightmares and

Julia ... Miss DuBois ... said she thought Althea might be using the psychic connection to send me nightmares."

"I see," De la Croix said. "And when did you become aware that you were not the only person the Rubidoux Coven had inflicted with the *loup-garou* curse?"

"When Miss DuBois and I went to look for Pixie Arrow mushrooms for the counter curse, we came upon some men hiding in a remote area of the swamp. They told us Althea had cursed them as well and they'd been hiding there to keep their friends and families safe."

"How many men did you find hiding out in the swamp that day?"

"Thirteen," Dalton said. He heard gasps from the people seated around him.

"And was one of those men Luther Rubidoux?" De la Croix asked.

"Yes," Dalton told the crowd. "That's who he said he was and the other men called him Luther and said he was Althea's own cousin." More gasps and hushed whispers went through the crowd of seated people.

"Did this man tell you how and why he came to be amongst the men there?"

"Yes, sir, he said he'd been sent there because he'd helped Althea to kill his mother so they could take over their coven, but that Althea had double-crossed him and had her people curse him and take him to the swamp in exile." Now, Dalton heard gasps and muttering coming from the people standing in chains. The staff pounding on the floor quieted most of those speaking, but Dalton heard women weeping nearby.

"How did Mr. Rubidoux say he'd brought about the death of his mother?"

"He said Althea had given him a box of chocolates laced with Pixie Arrow poison and he in turn gave them to his mother. He admitted that he watched her die of the poisoned chocolates. He then took the Rubidoux ritual chest to Althea, and was accused by her of killing his mother and cursed with the *loup-garou* by the coven as punishment." Angry voices could be heard from the crowd, condemning Luther and Althea alike.

"And where," De la Croix shouted above the angry onlookers, "is Luther Rubidoux now, Mr. La Pierre?"

"He's dead. I don't know where his body is, but he went with five other men who'd been cursed and had already made more than twelve turns into the beasts to collect Pixie Arrows for us, so we could make the counter-curse. They gave their lives to help us rather than make the change again. They collected the poison mushrooms without protection for their hands, poisoning themselves in the process."

"To your knowledge, Mr. La Pierre, were the thirteen men you met the only other victims of the curse?"

Dalton was, at first, hesitant to answer. He'd watched enough Law and Order episodes to know this testimony would be hearsay evidence, but taking in his surroundings, he didn't think the same rules of law governed these proceedings. As far as he could see, the defendants didn't even have representation and Dalton didn't know how he felt about that.

"We were told by one of the men that there had also been two women who'd been turned, but they'd been killed during the full moons after being in fights with the males. I can only assume you are going to be getting testimony from those men, as well."

"Yes, of course, Mr. La Pierre. The others will be giving their testimony here tonight. Thank you. You may return to your seat." De la Croix dismissed him, turning his broad back. Dalton stood up to return to his seat next to Julia. Before stepping down, he glanced over to see Jerry staring at him and gave the little man a reassuring nod. The frown, however, never left Jerry's face.

As the night wore on, all the men from the glen were called to give testimony along with Julia, Ruby, and Melanie DuBois. Tom and Peg also gave testimony about finding Bernard and Terry's bodies and the strong Residual lingering upon them. Julia related Althea's admission on the dock about why she killed them and how. The heart-wrenching weeping of Melanie and Ruby during the testimony had to sway the judges against Althea, in Dalton's way of thinking.

21

As the clock struck three and echoed through the big room, the Herald announced the decision of the eight men and women paneled as judges in the matter. "After hearing testimony from all the injured parties involved, it is the High Council's decision that Althea of the Rubidoux and her former coven are guilty of breaking High Council Law and subject to the sentence of Antoine, head of the De la Croix Coven. The sentence will be given and carried out before dawn today. Mr. De la Croix, what say you in this matter?"

The Herald pounded his staff and Antoine De la Croix stood. "Fellow Coven leaders, it pains me to find it necessary to pass this judgement on another coven of my own region, but we have had Laws amongst us for centuries to keep ourselves in check against this very sort of thing. What the Rubidoux perpetrated could have cost our very secret society dearly had those cursed with the *loup-garou* not kept themselves hidden away as they did. The ban on that particular curse was placed for just that reason: to keep us and our many secrets safe from the outside world. Our oldest and most dearly held law, the Reade, was also broken. The Rubidoux caused harm to innocents with their magic by invoking those curses."

De la Croix stared directly at Julia DuBois. "I have recently been chided for considering a repeal of the Reade in Council, and have given the matter much thought since then. If we turn our backs on that one law governing our moral path, more of this"—he swept his big hand to indicate the defendants standing bound in lead upon the dais—"will continue to go unchecked, putting all of us and those we love in danger. We cannot come out of the Shadows yet, if ever." Loud murmuring could be heard from those seated, both in favor and against De la Croix's words. The staff of the Herald pounded on the floor and the room fell into reluctant silence once more.

"In the matter of Althea"—he deliberately refused to give her the Rubidoux name—"and the murder of Eleanor Rubidoux, her Coven Mother ..." The bruised and shorn woman was pulled forward from amongst her cowering fellows. "I sentence you to death in the manner in which you chose for your victim and by which your accomplice, Luther Rubidoux, met his end. You will drink a concoction made of the Pixie Arrow and stand before us while we watch you succumb. So mote it be! Herald!"

Althea stared ahead, refusing to look at De la Croix. Dalton almost felt sorry for her, and he could feel Julia shivering at his side. He reached over and took her cold hand.

The man who'd carried the heavy staff came forward with a heavy goblet in his hands. Dalton wondered if the goblet was made from lead. Another big man took Althea by the back of her neck and held her while the Herald put the cup to her swollen lips.

At first, Dalton thought the woman would take her punishment without fuss, but at the last moment, human instinct kicked in, and Althea began fighting and twisting her head away from the cup holding her death. Another big man joined them upon the dais and held Althea's thrashing head steady while the Herald poured the black liquid into her mouth. Much of it was spit back toward him and he dodged the deadly spray coming from between Althea's cracked lips. Dalton knew that even the

156

little bit running down her trembling chin was probably lethal. Some in the crowd laughed when the man tired of fighting her and threw the last bit of the poison into Althea's wide blinking eyes.

"You were, indeed, a sorry replacement for the beautiful and regal Eleanor Rubidoux. She may have been a woman small in stature, but Eleanor Rubidoux stood hand and foot above the likes of you, little girl," Antoine De la Croix spat. He then turned to the standing coven members, quaking behind their former High Priestess. "I have little sympathy for those of you who followed this spoiled cow, but I've taken council with my Coven Sisters. You followed the directions of your Coven Mother as was your sworn duty, misguided as it may have been.

"Your Coven has been stricken from the lists and you all go nameless now and are denied home in any other coven upon this Earth." A collective sigh of relief came from the bound group upon the dais as they realized they would not meet the same fate as Althea, but De la Croix was not finished. "Further, you will all wear lead bracelets and collars for the remainder of your days. All magic is denied you and those who see you will recognize your shame. So mote it be!" Men and women came forward and attached wide lead collars and cuffs to all on the dais and locked them with small padlocks, so they could not be easily removed by the wearers.

Dalton wondered how long it would take for the lead in the jewelry to leach into the wearers' systems and drive them mad or kill them with its toxicity. Jerry caught his gaze and gave him a weak, nervous smile. Dalton studied Althea and recognized the first signs of the Pixie Arrow taking hold of her. Sweat began to glisten upon her shaved head and run down into her once beguiling face, causing runnels to appear through the black poison still upon her cheeks. As she began to groan and cough blood onto her white robes some in the seats around Dalton looked away.

The men who'd administered the poison to Althea had raised

her shackled hands above her head and attached them to a hook bolted into the stark block wall. She hung there writhing in pain as the poison surged through her delicate system. The tawny skin of the woman had turned pale as she coughed and more blood ran from her abused mouth. Soon her blood, as it thinned beyond what her vessels could contain, began to ooze from Althea's ears, eyes, and from the very pores of her skin. Her white gown became saturated with the red fluid and clung to Althea's slim body, outlining the curves Dalton had once so enjoyed in her bed.

Blood dripped into and from Althea's dark, deep-set eyes. The tall, young woman began to gurgle and choke as her lungs filled, and she could no longer get a clear breath of air. She soon began to jerk and seize, her body writhing upon the hook until finally she took one last gasping breath, coughed out a mouthful of blackening blood and slumped dead in her chains. Everyone in the room gagged as the bloody young woman's bowels evacuated, filling the entire room with the foul stench of death when Althea evacuated her bowels on the floor beneath her dangling voice.

"The Big Kahuna certainly knows how to put on a show," Dalton mused. Julia elbowed him in his ribs.

The members of the former Rubidoux Coven were herded off the dais and through the crowd of onlookers who'd begun to stand. "What will happen to them now?" Dalton asked. "Will they just go back home to St. Elizabeth?"

Julia shrugged her shoulders. "Some might, but the island has been confiscated by the High Council. If they lived out there, they'll have to find new homes and most have lost their jobs if they had one."

"Did your High Council take its lessons from the Catholic Church or the other way around?" Dalton asked dryly.

He thought about Jerry and Lenny. The tow truck driver from St. Elizabeth doubted Wal-Mart would allow a checker to wear a wide metal collar or cuffs as part of the uniform. Lenny might be able to go back to his job at the marina, but somehow Dalton doubted it. An old man wearing strange jewelry might be tolerated in some places, but not in the conservative redneck fishing camp on the Vermillion.

Julia took Dalton's hand. "I love you because you have a big heart, babe. Those bastards cursed you, but you're still worried about them and how they're going to get by." She brought his tanned hand to her lips and kissed it. "You're an amazing man."

Dalton and Julia began moving along with the others out of the room. He saw Ruby walking with a pale, trembling Melanie pulled close to her.

"Do you really think that was something the kid should have been forced to watch?" Dalton asked, glancing again at the bloody corpse suspended from chains upon the dais. He suspected Althea was being left to hang until the room emptied as a final reminder of what crossing De la Croix could get you.

"She needed to see it for closure if nothing else," Julia whispered. "It will also give her pause if she ever thinks to use her power to do ill."

Dalton wiped at his nose, trying to erase the foul stench. "I don't suppose I can argue with that, but she's just a kid. That was a real-life horror flick. It could scar her for life."

"I'm gonna introduce Mel to Miss Amanda tonight and if she senses any trouble in her, Mom and I will bring her in to meet with her for a while."

"That's a good idea," Dalton said. He set a hand lightly upon Julia's abdomen. "Do you think watching that messed with *her* head any?"

"I don't think so, Dalton. Some things can't be absorbed in-utero."

"But what if Mel was giving her a play-by-play? Didn't you say that they *talk*?"

"You talk to her, don't you?" Julia asked, smiling warmly. "You get to be a dad way before most men do. Be a dad and check it out, but I think she's all right. I haven't been picking up any agitation from her."

"You mean like how she kicks when you eat green peppers or cucumbers?" Dalton chuckled as they began climbing the stairs back to the main level of the De la Croix mansion.

*"Marsha says she hopes you have some ice cream tonight."* Melanie cheerily said, using her telepathy

*"Any particular flavor?"* Julia asked, smiling down at her niece.

*"Not chocolate. Chocolate gives her a belly ache."*

*"Really?"* Julia rubbed at the small bump on her lower abdomen.

"I couldn't eat chocolate when I was pregnant with you *or* Bernard," Ruby added. "Neither of you spoke to me the way Marsha seems to speak to you, but you would both flop around and kick like little demons."

"Well, this one does plenty of that, too." Julia said, smiling. "I think she's going to be a gymnast."

They stepped out into a room much more festive than the one below. Tables lined the walls heaped with seasonal delights. Aromas of cinnamon and nutmeg filled the air. Melanie broke away from her grandmother to dash for a table with trays of caramel apples and popcorn balls. A string quartet played lively Celtic tunes and dancers in long gowns filled the center of a parquet floor.

"Now this is more like what I was expecting from a Witches' Ball in the Garden District," Dalton said as he made for a table with large glass punch bowls, smoking from the dry ice in the orange punch. "I'll get you ladies a drink."

"No alcohol for me," Julia reminded him.

*"Absolutely not,"* he called back to her telepathically.

"That boy is a pleasure," Ruby said, patting her daughter's arm. "Have you decided on a date for the wedding?"

"Winter Solstice." Julia took her mother's thin hand. "I've

always dreamed of a winter wedding done up in winter white, burgundy, green, and gold."

"You'll be a beautiful bride, but do you think you can put a wedding together in only two months?"

"Are you kidding?" Julia laughed. "I've been planning this wedding since I was twelve years old." Julia pointed to her head. "It's all up here."

"Of course, it is." Ruby said, then took the cup of punch offered by Dalton.

"Of course *what* is?" Dalton asked, offering a cup to Julia.

"Our wedding. It's all in my head." Julia took the cup from him and drank deeply.

"Oh, right," he sighed out and rolled his eyes. "I never would have thought witches would fantasize about faery tale weddings."

"I may be a witch, but I'm still a girl, and girls fantasize about their wedding days."

Dalton scooped up a small pumpkin from the nearby table, set it in the palm of his hand and bowed formally. "Your carriage, m'lady."

"Oh my," Ruby giggled.

"I hope you ladies are enjoying the festivities now that the pleasantries of the night have been attended to." Antoine De la Croix said from behind them.

"Thank you, Antoine." Ruby took the big man's hand. "I regret that your lovely party had to begin with such unpleasantness."

"The duties of a High Council leader are not to be shirked because they may be unpleasant." His eyes caught Melanie's blonde head at Dalton's waist. "I hope the young Miss was not too upset by the goings on downstairs."

"The Young Miss was not," Melanie spoke upon her behalf. "When I lead the High Council I will remember your strength and wise counsel here tonight, Mr. De la Croix."

De la Croix raised an eyebrow and smiled at Julia. "You will have your hands full with this one."

"The DuBois Coven will be in good hands when her time comes."

"Yes, it will," De la Croix said, laughing, "but strong women have never been a problem where the DuBois were concerned. I've made a point of studying your line and it is a long and noble one. My daughter, Amelia, gave birth to a strong son last year. Perhaps we should consider joining our houses with the birth of that one." Antoine De la Croix nodded to Julia's midsection and smiled.

"Wait a minute, now," Dalton interrupted. "Doesn't her dad have any say in this?"

"Not really, Uncle Dalton," Melanie informed him. "The mother makes those kinds of decisions in our society. Aunt Julia will choose which family to align Marsha with."

Dalton glanced at Ruby. "And you let her get stuck with me?"

"I gave up on trying to make decisions for my daughter long ago, Dalton." Ruby chuckled. "You will, too, if you want a peaceful marriage."

Dalton could smell the truth in Ruby DuBois's words. In the weeks since the lifting of the *loup-garou* curse, he'd been happy and a little worried to find that he hadn't completely lost his enhanced senses.

Until the first moon had passed without a change, Dalton had feared the possibility that the ritual hadn't worked. He could still smell fear, anger, and desire, as well as discern when someone lied or told the truth. Julia had told him they were senses he'd probably always possessed and that the curse had simply made him aware of them for the first time. Now that he was aware of them, Dalton would always be able to make use of them.

"Mrs. DuBois," Dalton said, smiling, "I've learned my lesson where crossing women and witches are concerned. Whatever my Jules wants, my Jules gets."

"You are a much wiser man than what I first gave you credit for, Mr. La Pierre," Antoine De la Croix chuckled in his deep voice. "Much wiser, indeed."

**THE END**

Dear reader,

We hope you enjoyed reading *Moon of the Witch*. Please take a moment to leave a review, even if it's a short one. Your opinion is important to us.

Discover more books by Lori Beasley Bradley at https://www.nextchapter.pub/authors/lori-beasley-bradley

Want to know when one of our books is free or discounted? Join the newsletter at http://eepurl.com/bqqB3H

Best regards,

Lori Beasley Bradley and the Next Chapter Team

You might also like:
Life Shadows by Lori Beasley Bradley

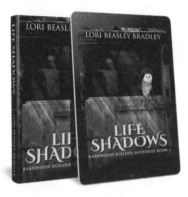

To read the first chapter for free, please head to:
https://www.nextchapter.pub/books/life-shadows

on Of The Witch
78-4-86751-381-1

hed by
apter
-Otsuka
u, Tokyo